THE LEGEND OF
HO-TA-WA

A Novel
By R. L. David Wood

Feather Valley Publishing
and Literary Agency, Inc.

Angola, Indiana

Dedicated To Our Son Charles

Who Is Still Young Enough To Like

A Good "Injun" Story

Chapter 1

Zeb Sullivan lay in a drunken stupor in front of the whiskey dealer's tent. It wasn't a tent at all, really, but just a few boards with ox hides spread over them. The mud from the spring rains was knee deep as whiskey hawkers yelled out their rot gut at fifty cents or two hides a shot.

Renegade Indians dressed only in breech clouts and feathers stood in line along with soldiers, French rivermen and fierce-looking men in buckskins, all waiting for one shot of the half coal-oil and corn mash whiskey. They were all laughing as Mary Lou Sullivan frantically tugged at her husband's long, skinny body, trying desperately to extract him from the mud.

Although Mary Lou was of hearty stock, her attempts were futile. She was an extremely pretty woman, evident even in her rough frontier garb of linsey woolen frock and bonnet. The lines of a well-formed woman were evident as she bent to retrieve her drunken husband from the mud.

The harshness of frontier life had in some respects taken its toll on Mary Lou, leaving only traces of the young woman who had been the daughter of a Boston merchant, with genteel upbringing and education at Miss Ambrose's School for Young Ladies. Zeb, too, bore little resemblance to the tall, curly-haired young man of ambition who clerked for Mary Lou's father.

The scene playing out in the rough surroundings recalled little of the young newlyweds who had responded to the call of the frontier twelve years earlier, a call leading them eventually to Virginia, Kentucky and now Cincytown. No one could have guessed that the two had once been so devoted to their dream of a new life in the frontier that they had been happy to leave the comforts of the big city behind and to bring their two children into the world in the most difficult of situations. It was Zeb's insistant drinking that had come to make the dream a nightmare. Any close observer could tell that the brood was held together mostly by Mary Lou's stubborness and perseverence.

As she tugged at Zeb's arm, it was evident that she was tired and her futile attempts somehow made her seem pathetic and without hope. The jeers of the assorted scum made little difference to Mary Lou, for they had become a daily part of her life. Her attempts to get Zeb up and home, though, were for Danielle and Aaron's sakes only. Long ago, Mary Lou Sullivan had stopped caring.

"Please, Zeb. Get up, please. The children are tired and we best be gettin' home to our milk cow. Zeb, *please* get up!" Again she tugged, while the ragged bunch of hangers-on laughed.

"Ah, Pierre, see zee drunk? Hey, Madame. Leave heem be. Come. Come with me. Labeau promises he will show you a great time!" The French riverman reached for Mary Lou's arm. A hard hand tightened around her wrist while the assorted frontier ruffians laughed. Mary Lou jerked her arm, but the grasp was too strong.

"Let my Maw go! Let her be!" Aaron Sullivan, with all the fury of his nine years, charged at the Frenchman, his fists flying in the wind, while his sister, Danielle,

screamed. "Leave our Maw be! Leave her be!!" Mary
Lou screamed, too, as the hand closed tighter on her
wrist.

"Ah Ha, Labeau. You have to fight for it thees time.
See? The leetle one has a blade." Pierre laughed while
the ruffians moved forward towards the makeshift bar.

Labeau had seen the jack knife in Aaron's small
fist, and the look in the nine-year-old's flashing blue eyes
showed no fear. "I'll kill you, you polecat!" Aaron
yelled. "Leave my maw be or I'll kill you!" The Frenchman's free hand slapped out so quickly that the blow
fell before the young boy could see it coming. He could
hear his mother's screams as he landed backwards in the
mud.

"That'll be about enough, Frenchy. Let the lady
go!" The throng of frontier drunks grew quiet as a man
in buckskins stepped among them, facing the large
riverman and his prisoner. He was well over six feet tall
and lean as a young hickory, with sandy hair and a face
leathered by the elements. There was no belying his
trade. The buckskins were worn slick and had long ago
turned black from camp fire smoke and bear grease,
while at his Kickapoo belt hung scalp plews, telling of his
encounters with many an Indian buck.

"Ah Ha! What is thees we have here?" The Frenchman's glare never left the frontiersman's face. "Is thees
woman yours?"

"Nope. Reckon not, Frenchy. As I see it, that there
fellar wollowin' in the mud belongs to her. So why not
jest let go her arm and back off."

Mary Lou Sullivan was trying to get to her son, but
the grip had tightened.

"Zat drunk ees not fit to be thees purty woman's
man. So go away before I spleet you," the Frenchman

said, as he drew the long bladed river knife from his belt. "Pierre, come. Hold thees woman."

"Pierre, I'd advise you to stay where you're at unless you want to stand at the gates," said the frontiersman, the Flintlock 48/40 leveled at the breast of Pierre's body.

"Come, Labeau. Let her go. Come. Let's have whiskey," said Pierre. It was apparent that he knew the frontiersman was not joking.

Labeau bristled. "Ah, so thees skinny one has you scared, 'eh Pierre?" Labeau's knife arm suddenly and deftly drew backwards.

The muzzle loader was loud and the impact of the ball drove Labeau into the whiskey tent as Mary Lou Sullivan scrambled free.

"Hey. What goes on out there?" A yell came from inside the whiskey tent.

The frontiersman stood stock still, his grey eyes searching each man. No one moved. Deliberately, he began to walk towards the crowd as each one stepped aside to let him through. Then quietly the tall stranger stooped and, with one deft movement of his arm, he picked up Aaron Sullivan.

"Come on, Ma'am. Where's your buggy?"

Mary Lou looked at her husband. "We don't have a buggy, Mister. We're walkin."

"Makes no mind. Yonder's my horse. You and your younguns take him. Where abouts might you all live, Ma'am?"

Mary Lou was still watching Zeb. She looked forlorn and tired, dark circles beneath the warm brown eyes. A bitter look crossed the frontiersman's face as he surveyed the scene and watched the two rivermen pick up the dead Labeau and carry him towards the river. Death was an everyday occurance at Cincytown.

"We live out on the Fort Miami trace, about three miles away," Mary Lou answered.

"All right, Ma'am. I can find the place. You go along now. I'll bring your man." The stranger shoved the boy towards his Mother and moved back into the crowd to pick up Zeb Sullivan with ease. "Go along now," he said. "I'll follow."

Mrs. Sullivan and her two children, without a word, walked towards the Indian pony tied to a bush. Aaron kept looking backwards. There was amazement and worship in his eyes.

The cabin was nothing more than a lean-to, and a bony old milk cow stood in a pole corral bawling to be milked as the stranger deposited Zeb Sullivan on a pine bough rack. There was resentment in his eyes as he looked down at the drunk.

"Well, Ma'am. I guess that's about all I can do. You all be alright?"

"Yes, Sir, Mister . . . . uh, my goodness. I don't even know your name. But I surely am grateful to you for helpin' me and the younguns."

"Name's Allen Crosstree, Ma'am." He looked embarrassed. "Some folks calls me Ho-Ta-Wa."

Mary Sullivan tried the Indian name. It didn't come out like Allen Crosstree said it, and they both laughed. Mary Lou noticed the stranger's strong white teeth and clear grey eyes that crinkled as he smiled.

"What's that name mean, Mister? Is it an honest Injun name?" It was Aaron speaking.

Mary Lou colored slightly, bringing a healthy glow to her cheeks. "Hush now, boy. Don't you be askin' strangers personal questions. Go now and milk old Bossey. It's clear she's hurtin', son. You too, Danielle. Now scat. There's evenin' meal to fix."

"But Maw. He's an Injun fighter. . . ."

"Hush, boy. Now go do your chores before your paw wakes up." Mary Lou's quick look at Zeb, as he stirred on his side to puke, revealed revulsion and a trace of fear.

"It's all right, Ma'am. The boy don't mean no harm. Tell you what, boy. You go milk that cow and if'n it's alright with your Mama and since I'll need to make camp, maybe I can camp over in the grove of woods and after supper you and me can pow wow." Ho-Ta-Wa looked at Mary Sullivan.

"Why, we'd be right pleased to have you stay over, and you could take vitals with us. Isn't much, but you're welcome."

"Gee willakers, Maw. Can I go over to his camp? Please Maw?" Young Aaron was excited, and his Mother realized she hadn't seen him that way in a long time.

"Land sakes, son. Go milk that cow. Then we'll see. Now scat!"

"Yes, Ma'am!" and young Aaron fairly ran toward the pole corral.

Allen Crosstree was tired and he wasted no time making camp, preparing his simple meal of oats and bear jerkey peeled from his buckskin pouch. He had politely declined to take vitals with the Sullivans for several reasons. He knew they were dirt poor and extra food was scarce. The winter of 1783 had been a cruel one. Even government troops had starved at Fort Miami during repeated Indian attacks by the Miamis, Potawatomies and Kickapoos. Old Chief Little Turtle meant to get the white man's butt clean out of the Northwest Territory. Supply lines were closed off coming out of Pittsburg Fort, so Allen knew that Cincytown hadn't faired any better. Anothe reason was Zeb Sullivan. Allen knew that Sullivan would awaken from his drunk humiliated and madder than a wet coon and a strange man at his cabin sure wouldn't help his disposition any.

The sun had set and off in the distance Allen could see the fire's glow from Cincytown. The drunks would now be spoiling for a fight and Allen Crosstree was glad to be alone. Occasionally, he could hear shouts from the Sullivan cabin. It sounded like Zeb had finally came around. Now there would be hell to pay.

Mary Lou was crying as she scrubbed the wooden bowls.

"Lord God, Zeb. What will we do? No cow. No farm. Why did you gamble it away? What about these younguns, growin' up here on the frontier with no home?"

"I know, Mary Lou. I know. I ain't got no excuse. I just thought I could win."

"Zeb Sullivan, that's what you said in Virginny and again at Fort Pitt. Now here. Where will we *go*?"

"Well now, just calm yourself. We're goin' to Fort Miami out on the Saint Mary's River. I've got us a wagon and horse. Now don't you fret. It'll be a new start. Washington's lookin' for settlers. They promised ten acres."

Mary Lou turned. There was fire in her eyes. "Fort Miami? My God, Zeb. There's hundreds of redskins between here and there, and chances are we'd never make it! Don't you remember what happened to that whole company under Captain Taylor? All dead—massacred by those savage Indians. And what wagon? What horse? We haven't got any money!"

"Now Mary Lou, you jest calm down. Ain't no use

yellin'. Hell, I made me a good deal with Jim Coogan.''

"Jim Coogan! You mean that whiskey sellin' trash?" Mary Lou threw the wooden spoon across the room, fire in her eyes.

"Yes, damn it. Jim Coogan. Now hush. The deal's all made. I clear his land for one year. Then we take up our holdin's. All you and the kids gotta do is tend us a garden and Coogan will give us a cow. We's leavin' first light tomorrow, and there ain't gonna be no more arguin about it.''

"Whoopee! Whoopee! We's goin' to Fort Miami!" Aaron and Danielle yelled and screamed as they ran from the cabin towards Allen Crosstree's fire. Mary Lou was too upset to stop them.

Allen stood as the two youngsters came running. "Whoa, there, you two woods colts. What's all the ruckus about?"

"We're goin' to Fort Miami, Mister Crosstree! We're goin' to Fort Miami!" Aaron was smiling from ear to ear and Danielle was watching the frontiersman intently.

Allen sucked at his Indian clay pipe as he spoke.

"Fort Miami, huh? And when's all this takin' place?" There was concern on his face.

"Why, we's leavin' tomorrow," Aaron answered. "Yes, Sir. At first day, we's leavin'.''

Well now. That'ds a fer piece to walk.''

"We ain't walkin', Mister Crosstree. Our Daddy's a'takin' Jim Coogan's plains wagon.''

"Is your Pa up and about boy?" The look of concern sharpened on Allen's face as he stooped and picked up his Flintlock.

"Yes Sir. He be up," Aaron answered.

"He ain't feelin' too well, though," Danielle answered.

"Well, then, come along. It's best me and your Pa had a little pow wow. Allen Crosstree started towards the cabin, the two Sullivan children trying hard to keep up with his long strides.

"Mister Crosstree, how'd you call that Indian name?" Aaron was practically running to keep up.

"Ho-Ta-Wa, boy. It means, in Kickapoo, Silent Wind."

"Kickapoo! You mean them savages we heard that butchered all them soldiers?"

"The same, boy."

"Is you a Kickapoo, Mister Crosstree?" Danielle had stopped dead in her tracks when she asked the question.

"No, Missy. I ain't no Kicky. Nope, not hardly." Allen chuckled.

"Well, how'd you get that there name, Ho-Ta-Wa?" Again, both kids were running.

"Well now, it's a long tale. Maybe sometime I'll tell you. For now, you best run ahead and tell your folks I'm a'comin' in. Now get!"

The children broke into a run and as they drew ahead, Alllen could hear Aaron telling his sister, "you best leave that fellar alone. Did you see all them scalps? I'll betcha he's killed a whole passel of them Injuns. Gosh. Wouldn't it be fine if he'd go West with us?"

Allen Crosstree smiled and spoke to himself, "Might be, boy. Might be. 'Specially if Jim Coogan's a'goin' west." His eyes squinted to narrow slits in the moonlight and glowed like foxfire at Haskill's swamp. Yes, Allen knew Jim Coogan well, as far back as '62 when the Cherokees raided Frankfort Fort over in Kaintuck.

As Allen waited outside the Sullivan cabin, his mind went back to that summer in 1762. The Crosstrees had moved into Frankfurt Fort from Lemon's Crossing, a clearing on the Pitch Creek, about thirty-five miles from the fort. Old Henry McCoffney had built the fort to trade goods with the Indian tribes of the area and things were peaceful until that summer when Jim Coogan and his four whiskey hustlers arrived from the Spanish Fort at Saint Louie.

Ben Crosstree and his two sons, Dan and Allen, had come to Lemon's Crossing in '61 when the fur trade had opened up in England, but soon after their arrival, Allen's mother had died of the consumption. Allen could remember almost nothing about her except her beauty and gentleness. After she died, they had moved to the fort. Ben was a Boston man of learning, and Henry McCoffney had hired him to tend the books at the trading post.

Dan was fourteen and little Allen had just turned nine. Those days at the fort were happy times. The boys had made friends with some of the Indian children nearby and for hours they would ride their horses through the forest or swim in Pitch Creek, while bucks in their bright beads and feathers brought otter, beaver and bear skins into the post for trade. Wind of the English up north and their fight to gain the Northwest Territory seemed of little consequence in the Kentuck area, so no one thought much of the five men with their pack train who arrived from Fort Saint Louie.

Coogan was a big man, dirty and foul-smelling, as were his men. McCoffney had instantly mistrusted them and made no secret of it, telling them to camp outside the stockade. In a matter of weeks, a steady stream of Indian bucks began to trade with Coogan for whiskey.

Before many days, a band of Miamis appeared and it
was obvious they knew Coogan and his men. Coogan's
whiskey flowed while the Miamis constantly talked of the
warpath to the Cherokee and how the white eyes would
hang their hair on their totems. McCoffney tried to talk
to the local chiefs, but to no avail. At night, bucks
danced the dance of warriors while the stockade shut its
gates and men with arms stood guard on the parapets.
No longer were Dan and Allen permitted to go to the
villages of the Indians. Instead, they were locked in their
cabin inside the stockade walls at night.

It was May when the stockade was attacked by the
Cherokee, with help from the Miamis. They assaulted
the stockade gates for hours, taking a terrible toll, while
fire arrows showered the cabins inside. Dan was pressed
into fire service while the elder Crosstree mounted the
walls with McCoffney and his trappers. Little Allen
remained in the attack cellar beneath the cabin floor,
coughing and gasping for air as hot sparks showered
down on him.

Suddenly it grew quiet—deadly quiet—and the
little boy huddled deeper into the corner of the cellar.
From then until morning he heard occasional screams
above, and he could feel that the fire above was growing
hotter.

It was dalight when Allen climbed from his hiding
place. Burned logs partially blocked his way, but finally
he gained what used to be the upper floor. He choked
back a cry. The cabin was completely burned down, as
was the entire stockade. Allen could see clear to the Pitch
Creek because there no longer was a front wall.

Tears began to slide down the smut-dirtied cheeks
as he desperately searched for his father and brother.
The dead lay in different positions. Some were mutilated

beyond recognition. All had been scalped, including Ruby Smith, the indentured girl who did McCoffney's laundry and kept the store clean. Her hair had been ripped off and her throat slit. The little boy stood frozen at the sight. Off in the distance he could hear the Indian braves screaming and yelling.

The elder Crosstree had been nailed to one of the main gates and when his son Allen found him, the boy stood motionless. He did not cry out, but stood silently crying. "Daddy, Daddy." Ben Crosstree had been stripped naked and skinned, just like a beaver or muskrat. Then his hair had been raised. Alongside him on the opposite gate hung McCoffney—only he had been split open and fox furs had been crammed into the open slit. Allen bit his lip until it bled, but he did not cry out.

Dan Crosstree had been lost to the fire, and as Allen surveyed the situation he became certain that the Indians would be back. He had come to realize, with a horrible sinking feeling, that he was the only one left alive.

He had no idea where to go or what to do, but one thought was paramount in his mind. He had been told that the Pitch Creek ran into the Cumberland. McCoffney used to say, "they joined together at Paradise." So Allen Crosstree, aged nine, with a sack of jerkey, struck out down the Pitch. A huge skinning knife that he had picked up at his dead father's feet was his only weapon. His experience in the frontier included one year of listening to the trappers tell tales, but he was determined to make it to Paradise. His last look at the now burned-out stockade cut deep into his mind. Corpses of friends and family lay strewn across the ground, and scattered among them were the clay whiskey pots of Jim Coogan and his men.

The shout from the cabin door inviting him inside brough Allen abruptly back to the present. As his body framed the cabin door, he could see that the Sullivans had been arguing. Zeb sat at the stump table while Mary Lou's back was turned towards the visitor.

"Come, sit down and have some coffee." Zeb motioned towards the rickety old saw horse chair. Allen declined with a nod.

"I surely want to thank you for helping my woman and younguns. Guess I got too much to drink." Zeb looked embarrassed as he spoke.

"It's all right, Sullivan, though I'd be a bit more careful about who I drink with. Your missus weren't havin' no easy time of it."

"Yes. She told me. I'm sorry you had to kill that fellar. Jim Coogan'll be mighty upset about that. Labeau was his head riverman."

Allen straightened. The look on his face showed anger, but years on the frontier had taught him to hold his emotions in check.

"Tell me, Sullivan. Is this here Coogan a big man?"

"Yep. That's Jim Coogan. Big and meaner than a bitch buffalo. Why? Do you know him?"

"Well, seems I seed him some years back—out of Saint Louie, ain't he?"

"The same. He's a trader."

"He's no trader, Zeb. He's a wiskey dealer a'sellin' that rot gut to whites and Indians alike!" Mary Lou's voice carried scorn.

"Now you just hush up, Mary Lou. You know there ain't no call to carry on like that. You don't let Jim Coogan hear them words!" Sullivan's fist slammed down on the table.

Allen felt sorry for the woman and kids. He

reckoned the litle boy, Aaron, was about the age he was when his brother and father were massacred.

"Ain't no need to get riled, Sullivan. From what I hear, Coogan ain't no saint. But that's your business. I hear from the younguns that you're goin' to Fort Miami. That true?"

"Yep. It's a fact. We's leavin' tomorrow at first day."

"Well, it ain't none of my affair, but I just came from out that way and I'd think it over a'fore I'd take these younguns and your woman across the trace. Hell, it ain't even safe here in Cincytown since Little Turtle and his braves joined up with the Prophet. Them's the meanest critters alive right now."

Mary Lou handed Allen a mug of coffee, her natural graciousness overtaking her anger. "Sit down, Mister Crosstree, and drink your coffee."

"Thankee, Ma'am," said Allen, as he hunkered down next to the wall. Aaron Sullivan imitated him by doing the same.

Zeb sat up straight. "You been to Fort Miami?"

"Yep. Jest got in last night. Hired on as a special courier for Wayne, deliverin' messages for the army."

Tell me is it true there's free land out there? Is mad Anthony Wayne a'givin' ten acres to settlers like I heered?" Zeb's voice was excited.

Allen looked disgusted as he spoke. "Yep. It be true. But you ain't gonna live long enough to clear it. Hell, the five nations has already begun to meet up. There's gonna be a Indian war, be my guess, and if I'm right, that fort's gonna be attacked.

"Well, they's soldiers there, ain't there?" Zeb seemed to be trying to defend his decision.

Allen stood. "They ain't many of 'em soldier.

Mostly they's drunks and volunteers. Old Wayne's might hard-pressed to keep 'em there."

"Well, don't make no mind. We gotta move on. Hell, I lost this place to Coogan at cards. We's *gotta* go!"

"We don't have to do any such thing, Zeb Sullivan!" Mary Lou spoke sharply. "If you was man enough, you'd go into Cincytown and tell Coogan you want your place back. We all know you was cheated!"

"Hush up, Mary Lou! You ain't got no call to talk to me that way in front of the younguns and this here stranger."

Danielle and Aaron looked uncomfortable, and Mary Lou angrily threw aside the blanket and stepped into the lean-to bedroom.

Allen sat his mug on the table. "Well, best I be goin'. I'd think about what we poke of, Sullivan. Thank your woman for me."

"Wait, Mister Ho-Ta-Wa! You promised to tell me about them Kickys that named you!" Aaron said, as he jumped up.

"Ho-Ta-What?" Sullivan asked. "What's this about savages?"

"Ain't nuthin', Sullivan. I was jest talkin' to your younguns about my Injun name."

"Crosstree . . . . Crosstree," Zeb Sullivan kept repeating the name until recognition lit up his face.

"Now I know where I heered it! Crosstree. Weren't you that fellar that was taken captive in '63 by the Kickapoos? Sommers down in Kain-tuck weren't it? Somethin' about them namin' you 'Silent Wind'. You that same fellar?"

Allen was nonchalant in his answer. "The same. I be the same, I reckon."

"Well, I'll be horn switched! Ain't you the fellar

that warned the Haskill train not to go through from
Fort Miami to Fort Dearborn two years ago?"

"Yep. But didn't do no good. Whole train was
massacreed over by Mongo Crossin' at Pigeon Creek."

Now Sullivan's voice grew belligerent as he puffed
out his chest and looked from his children to Allen.
"Yep. Reckon you's the same man. You lived with the
Kickys, didn't ya? Hear tell that there was some talk
about you leadin' some of them savages."

Allen tensed. The long rifle came up slowly. "Easy
there, Sullivan, with that talk. Ain't no man ever called
me traitor to my face."

Zeb was obviously a coward. "Ain't no reason to get
riled, Crosstree. It was just talk that I was repeatin'."

"Well, many a man's got his innards took out over
talk, so I'd advise you to be careful. I'll say my goodbys
now to your younguns. You be good, children, and tell
you Mama thank you for me." Allen delibertly took no
more notice of Zeb Sullivan, and as he stepped into the
moolight, he vowed that he, too, would be going to Fort
Miami come first day.

Chief An-To-Wee stood tall and menacing as he
faced the great chief, Little Turtle of the Miamis.
Painted warriors sat in a circle around the bright fire
deep in the forest at Mongo Crossing and, as the chief
spoke, all eyes were upon him.

"You say, Little Turtle, that if the Kickapoo join
your war against the white eyes that the territory from
the Saint Mary's to the land of the lakes and toward the
rising sun to the Fort at Defiance shall be ours?"

"It is true, Shooting Star." The Indian translation
for An-To-Wee was used by Little Turtle. "The area
known as buffalo trace will belong to you and your

people, so that your old women and children shall eat and rest in peace. When we are victorious over the white eyes and drive them from our lands, they shall no more capture your maiden squaws and kill them!"

Little Turtle handed the buckskin packet to An-To-Wee and stook back. "Here it is, Shooting Star, the proof of what these mad white eyes have done. It is this I have summoned you for."

An-To-Wee's eyes narrowed slightly as he took the packet, distrust evident on his face. Opening it carefully, he suddenly knelt, tenderly removing the squaw scalp plews luxurinatly braided with the Kickapoo beadwork. The chant of mourning rose in his throat and drifted out over the evening air—a lonely, forelorn sound. All were silent, and bowed their heads in respect for the great chief's grief.

After a long time, An-To-Wee rose again to his feet. "Where did you find this, Little Turtle?" he asked.

"My braves took it from white scouts who shot at them. They battled and killed the scouts, who wore the uniforms of soldiers at the Fort called Miami."

"What is it you want from my tribe, Little Turtle? My heart is heavy."

"Join us, my brother, in fighting these white eyes. In a few days we attack the fort. We want the Kickapoo to ride with the Miami, the Sauk and the Shawnee."

"But what of your treaty with the whites, Little Turtle? Are you of the forked tongue?"

Little Turtle stood. "I, Little Turtle, made no such treaty! It was Yellow Bear of the Potowatomis who spoke in my absence. The whites at Fort Miami have killed two of your Maidens. They are taking our land. They have driven away those who once traded with us for furs. When we drive them out, the English traders can return.

If not them, there are black beards at a place called
Saint Louie who will trade with us. Our tribes can again
prosper, can again hold the land that is rightly ours."

"A war now, Little Turtle? Many braves will die,
braves we need. The Fort will not fall easily."

"More easily than you think, Shooting Star. There
are leaders of the long knives in the Fort called Miami
who meet with the black beards even now. They will open
the gates for us when we attack. The battle will be like
picking berries, and few of our braves will be lost."

"But the leaders of the fort," An-To-Wee
responded, "they are of the white leader across the
mountains. How is it they are also of the black beards?"

"Because they are white eyes, my brother. They do
not understand honor. I myself tortured the Shawnee
runner who carried the magic paper to Coogan at the
Fort on the great river, and I know this is true. They are
forked-tongued like the snake. The white man must die!
Now!!"

Little Turtle's braves screamed the cry, "War!
War! War!!"

An-To-Wee spoke at last, holding up his hands,
palms down. "We of the Kickapoo must not let our
maidens be killed without reason. We will fight. But we
will fight alone. We do not need the Shawnee, the Sauk
or the Miami. We will smoke your pipe and pass the war
belt with you on one condition."

"And what is that?" Little Turtle asked.

"On the promise that we have whiskey and guns
and that we avenge the deaths of these our children."

Little Turtle smiled. "Then it will be as you ask.
Soon Coogan will leave the Fort on the great river. We
are to attack his train, but we must make certain he and
his men escape. One of his wagons will be loaded with

fire water."

The pipe passed as warriors danced the dance of
death and screamed their definance of the white men.
The Indian War of '83 had now been officially started
somewhere between Mongo Swamp and the Pigeon
Creek, while Coogan's train prepared to leave Cincytown
on the Ohio River.

Chapter 2

Allen was tired and hungry as he reached Fort Miami but he knew that he would have to set aside his personal comfort. An Indian war was already in the making and he would have to warn General Wayne.

As he approached Wayne's quarters, Lieutenant Price was coming out. The Lieutenant was tall, blond, and to Allen's thinking overly military. He'd never liked the man.

Lieutenant Price deliberately blocked the doorway as he spoke.

"Mister Crosstree, I thought you were in Cincytown! Can I help you?"

Allen stopped, eyeing the Lieutenant. "Was. Need to see the General."

"Sorry, Sir. The General's down sick with the flux. Blamed country. Sure takes it out of a man. You'll have to report to General Wilkerson."

Allen studied the Lieutenant for a long moment as he thought on it. Wilkerson was General Wayne's aide and ever since Taylor's Massacre, Allen hadn't like him. The General had hinted that Allen's Indian adoption divided his loyalty. Allen had also heard several rumors about Wilkerson that made him cautious.

The Lieutenant was insistant. "If you have dispatches or a scouting report, you'd best let General Wilkerson know now."

Allen turned without replying and crossed over the

parade ground to a small cabin. The sign on the door read, "Lieutenant General Wilkerson." Allen entered.

Wilkerson was fully dressed in parade uniform and the dark blue officer's coat made him seem taller than he actually was as he stood before the small fireplace. The sentry announced Allen to the General. "Sir, it's Crosstree, in from Cincytown."

Allen entered. "Come in, Crosstree. Come in. Thought you'd be in Cincytown enjoing yourself. What can I do for you?"

Allen stood straight, the grey eyes showing no feelings as he spoke. "I tried to see General Wayne. That Lieutenant Price says he's sick."

"That's correct, Crosstree. What's it all about?"

"Well, General, I came up on the trace and I run across a buck named Black Hawk."

The General interrupted. "That's one of your tribal brothers, isn't it? A Kickapoo, if I remember." The slur in the General's tone was unmistakable.

"Ain't no more, General. I had to put a knife in him. Here." Allen threw the Indian belt on Wilkerson's desk along with the fresh scalp.

"What's this?" Wilkerson exploded.

"That there, General, is Little Turtle's war belt." There was no mistaking the black and red beaded belt with the arrow emblazoned across the front. Allen continued. "General, this here pile of logs is about to be attacked."

"Preposterous, Crosstree! Why, just a few days ago I counciled with Little Turtle. I'd suggest you don't go around scarin' hell out of people with this talk."

"Well, General. Reckon how its your hide. But right now, a fellar named Coogan is on his way up the trace with a whole passel of red-eye likker. Seems like he

ain't comin' up fer trade since it ain't the fur season yet.
If'n I was you, I'd get this here belt to Fort Pitt and get
you some help—if'n it ain't already too late."

"Crosstree, don't tell me how to run my job! And
another thing . . . ."

Lieutenant Price entered. "Trouble, Sir?" he
asked, shooting a glance at Allen that showed contempt
and disrespect. Allen tensed.

Wilkerson repeated Allen's story. The Lieutenant
laughed. Allen stood, his right hand on his knife.

"General, ain't no sense to this. I've just come in
from scout myself. This man's a trouble maker."

Allen pulled the deadly-looking knife, his grey eyes
slits. "This here youngun is gonna get slit, General."

The Lieutenant backed up and General Wilkerson
spoke. "Tell you what, Crosstree. Hugh Applegate is in.
I'll send the war belt to Fort Pitt by him, In the meantime, let's keep this quiet so we don't panic the fort.

Allen kept his eye on the Lieutenant as he nodded.

"In the meantime, Crosstree, best you scout out
south and east of here."

"Cain't do that right now, General. I've got
somethin' else to attend to."

He felt uncomfortable and angry as he left the
General's quarters and crossed over to the post trading
building. Something was wrong. After a few minutes
thought, Allen made up his mind. He walked quickly up
the muddy grounds and again climbed the log steps to
General Wayne's quarters. A sentry barred his way.

"Sorry, Sir. No one permitted. Lieutenant Price's
orders."

"Get the hell outta the way, sonny. I aim to see
General Wayne." Allen shoved the sentry to one side and
entered.

General Wayne lay on a cot. There was no doubt that he had the fever.

"Beggin' your pardon, General," Allen apologized. The sentry entered. "General, I . . . ."

General Wayne spoke, interrupting the sentry. "Leave us alone, son." He waved the young man out. "Well, Crosstree, what is it?"

Allen was opening his mouth to answer when Lieutenant Price burst through the door. "What the hell *is* this, Crosstree? I said no visitors! Can't you see the General's sick?"

"It's all right, Lieutenant. It must be important. Sit down, Crosstree."

"Important, General! It's a bunch of damn nonsense he's come in here with!"

"You're out of line, Lieutenant. I'm gonna hear the man out."

Allen took a seat, but the Lieutenant continued to stand near the doorway, his anger visible.

Allen repeated what he had said to General Wilkerson.

"How'd you say you came by this war belt, Crosstree?" The General had asked the question before. Now he only wanted to be sure. The Lieutenant was openly hostile.

"Beggin' your pardon, General, but this here man's story don't hold water. Why, General Wilkerson just pow-wowed with Little Turtle nor more'n four days ago over on the Saint Joe. Little Turtle was goin' north to the land of lakes. You can't take no stock in these Injun squaw men."

Allen jumped to his feet, the skinning knife already in his hand. "I told you a'fore, youngun, to watch your mouth—or I'm gonna slit your tongue."

"Sit donw, damn it! Sit down, both of you!" The General's voice was surprisingly powerful, considering his weakened condition. He had propped himself up on his elbow and his look carried authority. "I won't have no bickerin' here," he continued. "It's bad enough with deserters, drunks and cowards. I don't need my officers gettin' killed. And you, Crosstree, put that damn knife away!"

Allen slowly sat back down, never taking his eyes off the Lieutenant. He didn't like Price and he was still having some strange suspicions, the same ones he'd had since arriving at the fort. Something was up. He just couldn't quite figure what it was.

The Lieutenant stood in the doorway, his face red with anger.

General Wayne obviously was feeling poorly, and he grew testy. "*Sit down*, Lieutenant! That's an order!" he yelled. The Lieutenant took the seat by the doorway.

"Now Crosstree, tell me again." General Mad Anthony Wayne was deep in thought as Allen again recountered is experience.

"Well, General, as I told you, I decided to come on back here when I heered of Coogan's train that was comin' up from Cinceytown. Seems like they was an awful lot of Kikka bein' hauled aboard them wagons when they was loaded, so I decided to kind of hang back a touch. At Greenville, they camped in and one of Coogan's scouts moved on ahead. So I just tagged along. He weren't more'n a couple of miles out when this buck steps outta the brush. I knew him right off. It was Black Hawks of the Kicks. Hell, he and me used to battle as kids when I was their captive."

The Lieutenant coughed and snickered and General Wayne shot him a hard look.

"Seems that Coogan's man gave Black Hawk somethin' more'n jest a drink of red-eye. Then Black Hawk, after he gets the package, just up and splits this fellar's head and raises his hair. Well, I decided right then that somethin' was wrong, so I followed that Injun over towards Mongo way. I was just about to take his braids when up shows a war party of Miamis. There was a Kick warrior with them and he had this here belt."

"Some of your relatives, no doubt. Huh, Crosstree?" Lieutenant Price's words were accompanied by a sneer.

Allen barely moved, but the Flintlock slowly tilted to point directly between the Lieutenant's eyes.

"General, I reckon the Lieutenant here has lived about long enough. Now either you muzzel him or I'm gonna put out his lights."

General Wayne looked neither shocked nor surprised. Slowly, he turned towards the Lieutenant.

"Lieutenant, I'm a sick man, but you ain't takin' advantage. Now I've given you fair warning. Mister Crosstree has my permission to blow your damned head off if you as much as even cough again. Is that clear, Lieutenant?"

Lieutenant Price looked like warmed over death as he stared straight down the bore of the 48/40. "Yes, Sir, General. Yes, Sir. I understand."

"Fine. Now please continue, Mister Crostrtee." Allen carefully held the rifle barrel level as he continued.

"Well, I saw the belt exchanged, but the packet went to the leader of the war party. I figured there weren't no way to get that package, so I went after the belt—since it was bein' carried by Black Hawk alone. Caught him south of here at Haskill's grave and put a knife in him. He sure put up a scrap, but weren't no use.

I left my mark so's they'd know it was me. I figured word would get passed on to An-To-Wee and maybe we could pow-wow about why one of his bucks would be carryin' the Miami war belt. Hell, he ain't never had no use for Little Turtle."

General Wayne lay for a long moment contemplating the scout's report. The he spoke.

"Crosstree, what's your connection with An-To-Wee? Are you close enough to get to him?"

"Well, General, cain't rightly say I am now. I've killed some of his braves over the years and they's been a price on my head ever since I left the tribe ten years ago. But, when I was a kid, we was real close. You know about him bein' . . . ."

The Lieutenant's expression showed ridicule when he put his hand up as if to cough but Allen's Flintlock steadied. Price's hand went down as the rifle tilted ever so slightly.

"As I was sayin', we was close once't, but you can't never tell about these Injuns, especially if they's likkered up. I could try, but I got somethin' else that needs doin' first. If'n I was you, General, I'd make sure Wilkerson gets that belt off to Fort Pitt like he said he would as quick as can be. My guess is these rag-tag soldiers ain't gonna last long in a major attack."

General Wayne tried to stand, but he broke out in a sweat and had to lie back down. After a few minutes he pointed to the large map of the Northwest Territory on the wall behind Allen.

"What if we sent a troop to Mongo Swamp and intercepted the savages there?"

"Hell, General, they'd know it the minute you left the fort. On my way in, I saw two Miamis in the Fort pretendin' to beg food. No, Sir. I'd get me a scout out to

Fort Pitt right away for some fresh troops. Then I'd close this place to all traffic. General, beggin' your pardon," as Allen spoke he looked straight at Lieutenant Price, "there's some that's a'wantin' this Fort to fall. To my thinkin' it ain't the English, so I'd say it was the Spanish that wants this here territory." The Lieutenant moved in his seat and Allen eyed him sharply.

"The Spanish? Hells fire, Crosstree. They're two hundred miles south!" The General's finger feebly pointed to the map. "They're clear down at Saint Louie."

"That ain't rightly so, General. "There's been some black beards just below the Kentuck border all summer, maybe closer from what I've heard."

General Wayne lay back for a moment, his arm across his eyes. Then he propped himself up again with difficulty. "Lieutenant . . ."

"Yes Sir, General." The Lieutenant asked permission with his eyes for Allen to let him stand. Allen nodded and the Lieutenant stood at attention.

"Yes Sir, General," he said again.

"Lieutenant, go fetch me Hugh Applegate."

"Yes, Sir. Right away, Sir." The Lieutenant departed, careful to close the door easy. His departing look still flashed anger at Allen.

The General managed a smile, even though he was obviously tiring from the meeting.

"You'll have to forgive the Lieutenant, Crosstree. He's inexperienced."

"It's all right, General. I jest don't trust him since Taylor's Massacree. Never could figure out how he outsmarted them Injun bucks."

"You tryin' to tell me somethin', Crosstree?" The General's look was quizzical.

"Nope, General, I don't claim to know about solderin' and the likes, but there has been some rumors about someone here in the fort and the Black Beards. I heard it in a village down at Cumberland. Fellar by the name of Boone claims he saw some big muckety-muck from Fort Miami along with Coogan all cozyin' up to them Spanish."

"Listen, Crosstree, don't you repeat this to anyone. I just sent a dispath to President Harrison about Wilkerson. Got reason not to trust 'im cause of some things that's happened here. In the meantime, I'll make sure that belt gets to Fort Pitt by Hugh Applegate."

"He's a good man, General, but tell him he sure better go north and east. Them trails south of here are plumb thick with Injuns and if'n I don't miss my guess, just about all of them are likkered up by now and ready to lift some hair."

General Wayne reached up to shake hands with Allen as the scout stood to leave. "Do what you can, Crosstree, to see if you can get to An-To-Wee. Hell, maybe he'll listen to you."

"Cain't promise you about that, but I'll do my best, General. First, though, there's a family travelin; with Coogan's train. I gotta see if I can get them through. There's a woman and two younguns. The man ain't much but I'd sure hate to see the hair of the woman and kids hangin' from a lodge pole."

"This woman somethin' special, Crosstree?" The General's eyes twinkled, though his smile was pale.

"Yep, she's right special," Allen thought, but when he answered it was casual. "Nope, General. Just folks tryin' to make their way. Jest thought I'd kinda look out for them."

The General smiled. "Well, then, best you get to it!

Tell you what. Bring them here and I'll see that they have a place inside the stockade. That way, you can go on about this other thing."

Allen nodded assent. "All right, General. Fair trade. They're only about a hard day's run from here by now. I'll jest mosey on down there and bring 'em in."

"What about the husband and Coogan? Won't they have somethin' to say?"

"General, if'n that woman wants to come with her younguns, there ain't no one gonna stop me from bringin' 'em in." There was determination in the scout's eyes.

As Allen Crosstree left the General's quarters, he could see Lieutenant Price coming out of General Wilkerson's hut across the parade ground. The two Miami bucks were seated on the wooden porch.

"Howdy, Ho-Ta-Wa. How be ye?" It was Hugh Applegate speaking as he came up the steps. He was a tall, weatherbeaten man, his white hair and beard wild and unruly.

In traditional Indian, Allen answered, "How!"

Hugh stopped and followed Allen's gaze across the parade ground. "Humm, two Miamis been a hangin' around for nigh on a week now, so I hear. Sure don't look like no starved Injuns to me." The old frontiersman spat at a crack in the porch floor as he spoke.

Allen turned. "Hugh, have you heard anything about an Injun uprisin'?"

"Well, I reckon I've heered a thing or two down about the springs." The springs Hugh mentioned were down the Miami River at Salt Lick Springs, a place where the water ran hot. It was the place where Indian brides went to soak themselves before the marriage dance, and it was also a place where frontier hunters rubbed their skins with sulphur water.

"When was you at the springs, Hugh?" Allen's question was deliberate, for it was there two days ago that he had raised the hair of the buck with the war belt.

"Let's see. I reckon by the sun, about two days ago. Sure was some activity there abouts. Bucks in paint comin' and goin'. It was then I found old Hayrake Johnson. Errer had gone plumb through his carcuss."

"Hayrake? You mean Hayrake's done cashed in?" There was disbelief in Allen's voice.

"Yep, Reckon he bought it. Least wise, I hope so, 'cause I dumped him in the springs. Didn't seem right to let some half-drunk Injun brave raise the old cusses hair."

Allen rubbed his chin. "Then it was his sign I cut just north of there. I ran down a Kickapoo with a war belt. The General has it now. Did ole Hayrake say anything a'fore he crossed over?"

"Yep. It weren't much, though, and sure didn't make much sense. . . . Land sakes, I can recollect when I first saw ole Rake, just like it was yestiddy. He'd jest showed up one day over by Fort Defiance with that right hand of his'n all bandaged. Said he'd cut them fingers off in a grist mill over by Chillicothe town. Turned out some fellar caught ole Rake and his lady together in a pole barn and the fellar jest ups and swings that hayrake and off comes Rake's fingers. Ever since that day, we all called him Hayrake." Hugh laughed a toothless laugh. "Long time and many moons since then. Way back in '59. Shucks. We was the first fellars that canoed across the Saint Mary's. Weren't nothin' here then except this here ole fort, but then it was all Frenchies, 'cept for some Injun squaws to help a fellar winter through."

Allen listened as if it was the first time he'd heard

the Hayrake story. Old Hugh loved to talk of the old times and Allen had a great respect for his kind.

Hugh spat as he spoke. "So you was the fellar that done the Frenchy in over in Cincytown, huh?"

Allen nodded. "Reckon so. You already heered about that, 'eh? What about Hayrake? What'd he say before he died?"

"Oh yea. Clean forgot. Well, he said somethin' about that cussed snake, Jim Coogan. Seems he saw Coogan feedin' some of his rot gut to some Kickys and Miamis down long the trace. Guess ole Rake hid in the bushes and heered them talkin' about Little Turtle and that back slappin' General called Wilkerson. About then, he cashed in."

Allen's voice had a tint of excitement in it as he asked his next question. "Hugh, there was a wagon train travelin' with Coogan. What about the train, did Hayrake mention the train?"

Hugh was silent for a long moment, studying the two Miamis across the parade ground.

"Hugh, the wagon train." Allen reminded him.

"Easy, sonny. Easy. I'm tryin' to remember. After eighty-four winters, a fellar's mind don't work none too fast. . . . Yep, he did say somethin' about a train. Somethin' about a massacree. Fellar by the name of Sullivan seems . . . ."

But the rest fell on the wind. Allen Crosstree was on a dead run toward the gate and, as he left the stockade behind, his mind was racing towards Mary Lou Sullivan and her two youngsters, Danielle and Aaron. His imagination was running wild as he hurried south on a seldom-used game trail parallel to the trace. He was too distracted to notice the two Miami bucks as they left the gate of the fort, running fast on a trail parallel to his own.

Chapter 3

Mary Lou Sullivan could smell the rot gut liquor loaded in their wagon and now, at high noon two days after they had left Greenville's cabin behind, they were still on the trace road. "Thank God," she thought, "that Fort Miami's only two days ahead." She was mad at Zeb, who now lay across the seat drunk while Aaron drove the team and little Danielle rode the lead mule bare-back. Up ahead, Coogan and his men laughed and yelled back insults.

The Martins had joined the troop for protection and their wagon had fallen in behind Zeb's. They were a nice couple and Mary Lou like Patricia Martin. At night they camped together and no one bothered them, simply because Abe Martin carried his Flintlock at the ready.

Zeb was always up at Coogan's fire drinking liquor, but Mary Lou no longer cared. She found herself thinking often of Allen Crosstree, and her feelings were confused. She felt deeply gratefuly to him for his help and she thought fondly of his boyish smile and genuine kindness. Yet she remembered how easily he had killed the riverman and it made her shudder. Such things were foreign to her and she didn't understand the killing, even though she had seen enough of it in her years on the frontier. She wondered why this Allen Crosstree could seem so gentle and yet so hard. What sort of a man was he? All she knew for sure was that he was unlike anyone she had ever known before. He had certainly left his

mark on the children, even in the short time they had
known him. Aaron constantly imitated Ho-Ta-Wa, even
in his pigeon-toed moccasin walk, and Danielle often
asked her mother if they would see the purty frontier
man at Fort Miami.

When the attack came, it was silent and without the
screams of the Indians. The forest on each side of the
trace was green and beautiful and they had seen deer,
bear and once a wolf. Birds had been singing, and the
fresh spring air made Mary Lou's spirits sing with them.
Then all of a sudden, there were no animals, no birds
singing and the mules were skittish. Mary Lou shoved
Zeb to the far side of the schooner's seat and called her
children to her, lifting Danielle onto the seat beside her.
The hair at the nape of her neck stood on end. Coogan's
wagon was moving too fast out front. Then it happened.

Zeb Sullivan was the first to die, as the flaming
arrow pierced his chest, but Zeb was drunk and as his
eyes opened they saw nothing. Slowly, he toppled off the
seat to fall beneath the wagon's great wheels. Danielle
screamed and Aaron grabbed for his father's old
Flintlock. Mary Lou shouted at the mules. "Heeah!
Heeah! Move, mules, Move!!" They broke into a headlong run.

The trace was rough with stumps and as Mary Lou
looked back, she could see that the Martin wagon was
already on its side. Savages were laying hatchet to
Patricia and Abe and their baby Sarah. Mary Lou's
terror became mixed with nausea as she turned to look
back at the trail. At that moment the wagon overturned
and everything went black.

Allen Crosstree abandoned his white self to take on
the keen characteristics of Ho-Ta-Wa as he ran the

forest trail. He had covered the distance in a day and a half without letting up and now from beneath his buckskin tunic he withdrew a deadly-looking hatchet. This he carried in his left hand and the Flintlock in his right. Bullets and patches were tightly gripped in his teeth while his moccasined feet skimmed across the trail. He knew instinctively that someone paralled him on the East trail but he reckoned he was safe from attack until he reached the Pigeon Creek area. Then he'd have to slow down, for it was there that they would lay in wait for him.

At Bennet's cabin, Ho-Ta-Wa stopped and stored both rifle and patch between the now burned-out logs. The Bennets lay buried over in the hickory grove. It seemd that nothing had changed in twenty years. The whites still came and the Indians still warred. There was no end to the coming and killing. It would soon be time for a man to move on—maybe even out beyond the English Fort at Dearborn or beyond the big creek.

The snap of the twigs instantly alerted Allen and quietly he moved into the now green foliage. Again the call of the owl. Now he knew his followers were close, too close. Quickly he bent to all fours, making his way through the brush. His grey eyes had taken on a flint look as they scanned every bush, every log and every mound of dirt. Finally they found their quarry. It was one of the Miamis who had been at the fort, and he stood in the shadows. Allen could see the black and orange war paint streaks of his face. There was no doubt what the Miami was waiting for, so Ho-Ta-Wa waited too.

Finally the second Miami joined the first. There was a hurried sign language exchange and Allen smiled as he translated in his mind.

"Are you sure it is he, Silent Wind, that we seek?"

"I am certain," the second replied by sign. "He has vanished."

The second Miami responded with deft finger movements. "We must find him. Remember the promise of Long Knife, the young one who wears the silver bars on his neck. This Ho-Ta-Wa suspects. We must find him."

The larger Miami looked angry. "He is like a ghost. Let us circle the old cabin sight. We must hurry. Soon the great chief Little Turtle will be ready." They turned towards Allen's hiding place.

The hatchet struck the larger Indian between the eyes and the blow carried him backwards into the other. It was then that Ho-Ta-Wa's knife found the second mark, neatly to the left of the arm pit. He stood perfectly still as the limbs of each savage thrashed out the last of life. Then quickly he lifted both scalps, tucking them still bleeding under his belt while he dragged the bodies beneath a dead fall. A squirrel chattered high above in a large oak.

Ho-Ta-Wa knew the springs were near as he slowly worked his way towards the trace. His nostrils picked up the burned smell of canvas, wood and flesh mixed with the sulphur smell of the springs even before he saw anything. He dreaded what he would find, but he forced his way forward.

One wagon lay on its side and he could clearly see the man and woman's bodies tied to the wheels. Both had been burned and scalped. He knew it was not the Sullivans. Still he stood quietly. He could be of no help to those already dead. As he scanned the trace, his eyes finally found the second wagon. No bodies could be seen and for the first time since he was nine, Allen Crosstree prayed.

There had been a scuffle. The boot prints of little Aaron Sullivan were still clear and there was no doubt in Allen's mind that the boy had been carried off. Silently and sadly he searched, but at first he could find no trace of Danielle or her Mother. Then he back-tracked the wagon, making sure he stayed off the trace. It was then he found Zeb Sullivan. A large hole was burned into his chest and his hair had been lifted. Allen felt no remorse, for he could still smell liquor on the body.

Patiently, Allen searched first south, then north, while the sun lowered in the western sky. Finally he found what he was looking for, a piece of gingham lay on a thorn bush. It was Danielle's or Mary Lou's. He cautiously skirted the area, becoming angry at his confusion. Then he made out a woman's shoe print mingled with the moccasion tracks of both Miami and Kickapoo, but his eye told him that the woman's tracks were fresher. A child's footprint indicated that she was being carried and occasionally set down. The answer to the mystery slowly unfolded to him. He cursed as he stood and watched the tracks. The woman, probably Mary Lou, was alone, wandering aimlessly.

Allen followed the tracks until it became too dark to see, and then his exhaustion overcame him. He knew he was off the main trail, so with care he crawled beneath a fallen ash to rest. As he lay there chewing jerky his thoughts began to dwell on the two Indians he had slain and on the Lieutenant back at the fort and chief Little Turtle's braves being on the war path. Was An-To-Wee also at war? This puzzled Allen, for he had cut Kicky moccasins on the trail. Knowing of An-To-Wee's long standing dislike for Little Turtle, he found it hard to imagine what could cause them to fight together. He fell asleep thinking of little Danielle being held captive at the

Kickapoo village.

The "Caw! Caw!" of a crow alerted Allen from his sleep. It was still dark, but ground fog had commenced to rise. Daylight lay only a few minutes away. The bird cry had come from the west somewhere near the trace and while Allen lay tense, waiting, another crow call answered back. It was the Kickapoo call and Ho-Ta-Wa knew exactly what it meant. At this moment the warriors were already moving towards their destination. So the Kicks were on the warpath. His mind was full of questions, but his main concern was Mary Lou Sullivan. He'd have to move fast to find her before a Shawnee, Kickapoo or Miami found her.

He had determined that by some miracle Mary Lou had gone free after the massacre, and he also knew that Aaron and Danielle had been taken, likely one by the Kicks and the other by the Miamis. Having been a Kickapoo captive himself, he knew that they treated their captives well, normally, but the Miamis would have no mercy. His chief concern now was to find Mary Lou before it was too late. If his calculations were correct, Fort Miami would be attacked before long.

Several hours passed with Allen moving fast and without sound through the forest, all of his senses keenly alert. The footprints led east and seemed to be meandering back and forth on a small game trail. The crow calls had steadily increased. Swiftly, half bent over, Allen continued to stalk the leather shoe print. He guessed she had moved slowly and aimlessly in the time since she had been out and, judging from the freshness of the footprints, she had covered little distance. He wondered if she might be hurt. In the trees ahead, he could see a sassafras grove, and suddenly he instinctively knew that something was wrong. Ho-Ta-Wa went to the

ground. The forest was absolutely still, but something or
somebody was in that grove. Gently and soundlessly he
removed the deadly hatchet. Then he tensed, frozen to
the ground. What he saw made his blood run cold. There
ahead, just to his right, stood a Delaware brave. There
was no mistaking the breech clout leggins with the otter
tufts down the sides. In his hand was a short war bow
strung tight with the sharp-tipped arrow. Allen could
not see the Indian's quarry, but he guessed, and the
thought chilled him. Slowly he raised to a springing
crouch. The distance was too far, but he had no choice.
He had to try and spring. There was no room to throw the
hatchet.

In mid-flight, Allen could hear the twang as the
deadly arrow left the tightly drawn thong. His arms laced
tightly around the Indian's knees, pulling him down. He
dared not look ahead at whatever the Indian's arrow flew
towards, but he had little doubt it had found its mark.

The buck was big and slippery, having, in tradition,
rubbed his body with bear grease. As he and Allen
thrashed in the underbrush, Allen was hard-pressed to
grab hold. Finding an opening, the Delaware sprang up
and back, facing his attacker. His bone knife came out
and the look of surprise at seeing the white eyes before
him momentarily cause him to pause. The instant pause
was just enough for Ho-Ta-Wa's hatchet to again find its
mark—but not a killing one. The blunt end of the
hatchet struck the Delaware dead center of the wish
bone and he fell like a tree. Allen sprung forward,
skinning knife ready, but he stopped short of trusting
the knife into the base of the neck at the spine. He hadn't
noticed before, but now it was obvious. The Delaware
wore no paint and at his side, neatly tied to his breech
clout, was a totem sack. A scout—an Injun scout. Allen

breathed out slowly, then quickly he cut the bag's thong and thrust it inside his buckskin shirt. Later he'd see what was inside. Right now, there was that arrow and its mark.

After tying the Indian's hands to his feet, Allen sprang into the grove at a dead run. He stopped mid-stride. His breath left him, and as he stared, his first emotional cry floated onto the air. "My God! My God, she's dead!" He was standing over the body of Mary Lou Sullivan.

She had slumped forward from a sassafras stump to the ground, the shaft of the arrow sticking outward near the shoulder. There was no movement and as Allen approached he could not detect breathing. He was in a rage and the thought to finish the job with the Delaware rose up.

Gently, the man of the forest turned Mary Lou over. Her face was scratched and the blood had dried, causing her to look as if she wore a strange smile. Allen winced as he grasped the arrow shaft, but he was also relieved. The arrow had penitrated the shoulder and was firmly imbedded in the socket. He knew it would have to come out if Mary Lou was to live, but at that moment, she was alive, barely.

Allen was concerned now. He knew that tribal warriors were all over, working their way east towards Fort Miami. But he would have to get the arrow head out and also he had to move—and move soon. The Delaware were in the area for one reason—to meet someone. Soon that someone would come looking.

Allen bathed Mary Lou's face tenderly and as gently as possible he made her comfortable, and stitched up her dress with rawhide. It had ripped open at her breast and as he laced it shut, his hands shook. Mary Lou was a handsome woman, and Allen had never before had these feelings.

   She moaned and suddenly her eyes opened, raw fear showing for a moment. Allen Crosstree was quite a sight to behold—unshaven, mud-streaked and blood, soaked. As Mary Lou looked down, her eyes fell on the two bloody scalps. She opened her mouth to scream and tenderly but firmly Allen placed his strong brown hand over her mouth, placing his face close to hers as he spoke. "Easy Ma'am. It's me, Crosstree. You've been stuck with an arrow. Easy. If'n you understand, nod. I ain't gonna hurt you. I came lookin' for you and your younguns."

   Mary Lou nodded as she sobbed and the hand came away. The brown eyes showed she was still terrified. "How . . . . how did you get here?" she whispered. "Where am I? My babies—oh my god, my babies! Are they all right?" Now she was trembling. Allen knew that he'd have to hurry. The shock from the arrow was beginning to take over.

   "Easy now, Mrs. Sullivan, easy. This here is a ticklish country we's in. There's Injuns all about so's we gotta be quiet." Then he lied. "Your younguns are all right, but first let's get that errer out of'n your shoulder. Do you understand?" She nodded. Her eyes were like a hurt fawn's and Allen bit his lower lip as he took up a sassafras limb and deftly cleaned it of its bark.

   "Now listen clearly, Mrs. Sullivan, I've got to cut that there errer out and its gonna hurt a might. So you jest bit down on this sassafras stick. It's mighty important you don't yell out. If'n you do, we could both wind up on a lodge pole. Can you do it?"

   Mary Lou looked at Allen long and intently, the pain showing in her eyes. But she was of good strong stock.

"Yes. Yes. I understand. Don't you fret, Mister Crosstree. I won't scream." As she bit down on the stick, she closed her eyes.

It was almost two o'clock by the sun and Allen was exhausted. The arrow had been difficult to get out and as he packed the open wound with sassafras leaves and pukey moss, he winced. It wasn't a surgeon's mark, but Mary Lou would live. He covered her gently, knowing that when she had fainted she would be out for a spell. Now he had other business at hand, namely one Delaware scout neatly tied and gagged.

The Delaware's hostility showed. He had been deprived of a scalp and thrust up like a dog, the lowest of humilitation for a brave. As Allen squatted before him, the muscles of the brave strained at the thong.

Allen knew the Delaware tongue and as he began to speak, the Indian relaxed a little. "Now you must be still and listen, oh brave Delaware." Allen pointed towards Mary Lou. "That there is my woman and I had no choice but to stop your play." Allen paused and the buck looked from Allen to Mary Lou. It was clear he understood and in the Indian villages no one coveted another man's squaw. It was the law. Finally he shrugged, making a gutteral noise from beneath his gag.

Allen continued. "I am known as Ho-Ta-Wa of the Kickapoo. An-To-Wee is my father." The buck was obviously confused, for this was no Kickapoo before him. Allen could see the doubt in the Delaware's eyes.

"Here, See?" Allen thrust his right thumb in front of the Delaware. The scar from the blood ritual was visible and the Delaware's eyes began to show understanding.

Next, Allen stood up a stick and drew a circle. He

jabbed a hole in the ground at Fort Dearborn. "Fort Dearborn. You know Chi-ka-go?"

The Delaware nodded.

Again, another hole. "Fort Miami. You know Fort Miami?"

Again the nod.

Then Allen jabbed a hole at the extreme opposite side of the circle. "Missouri River. Saint Lou. You know?"

The Delaware only stared.

In English Allen spoke, as he stared at the buck. "You sneakin' vermit. You know damn well that's your tribe's summer grounds. Now best you answer this next question or your squaw will be rubbin' ashes in her hair.

Allen took out the totem pouch. Inside was the white man pen stroker and seal on a yellow paper. Allen broke the seal as the Delaware began to struggle against his bonds. His open palm shot out and the slap, the lowest of insults, struck flush on the buck's cheek. In Delaware, Allen spoke. "You snake. You be quiet or I'll slit your stomach and pack it with earth worms." The Delaware quieted. The grey eyes were fierce and provoked fear. The letter was addressed to General Wilkerson and it read:

"You are instructed to cooperate with one Jim Coogan.

When Fort Miami has fallen, you are to dispatch your

Aide, Leiutenant Price, to the forks of the Cumberland.

There it will be arranged for our troops to move north."

Allen had been reading with difficulty. The

markings were strange to his eyes, and reading was not easy for him.

"We have deposited to your account the sum agreed upon at our last meeting and your station as territorial governor has been agreed upon in Madrid.

> In the Name of His Majesty
> Emperor of Spain
> General Adjutant,
> Amillo Castella"

Allen whistled under his breath, then spoke in a whisper. "That sneakin' polecat! So Wilkerson has caused the uprisin'. Well, reckon General Wayne would be mighty interested in this here letter. Allen folded the paper and tucked it in his own tote bag. Then he looked straight into the eyes of the Indian buck and again he spoke in the Delaware tongue.

"Who are you to meet and where? And why ain't you in paint? Is the Delawares takin' up the trouble path?" The Delaware knew that his answer would either spare him or separate him from his topknot. He indicated for Allen to removed the gag.

"All right, friend, but let me put it right. If'n you so much as breathe too hard, my woman over yonder will dress your hair." The knife came up point first, while Allen's right hand roughly jerked the buckskin gag down.

The Delaware spoke for the first time. There was no doubt that he was a brave Indian, but his look at the knife convinced Allen that he didn't take to the idea of dying so far from home.

"I am Little Fox of the Ohio Village. My people have been on the great buffalo trace to the Missouri where the black beards are camped. We are not at war, but the black beards have promised to feed our people during the white rains if they moved to Fort Miami on the Saint Mary's River. I was given ten ponies to carry the white man's paper.''

Allen interrupted. ''Was you in on the train massacree?'' His voice was low and soft, but the Delaware knew a lie would be detected.

''No, but I watched it from the great green trees with hair.'' Allen quickly calculated that he meant the mimosa trees near the springs. The Delaware continued. ''The dark ones attacked the last two wagons. The lead wagon was allowed to go forward.''

Again Allen interrupted. ''There were two Ha-tees. What became of them?''

The Delaware tensed before he answered. ''The dark ones caught the man child and two braves carried him away from the wagon road.''

''Which way did they carry him?'' The slate-grey eyes never left the Delaware's face.

The Delaware nodded his head east. ''Toward the new sun.''

Allen held his hand up for the Delaware to stop while he thought. That must mean that the Miamis have a war camp over near Defiance. That would be where they were taking the boy.

Allen nodded. ''Go ahead.''

The buck continued, ''The little squaw was also taken, but a large chief of another tribe claimed her. I heard his name called An-To-Wa or like that.''

Allen spat, ''Damn. Old Daddy hisself.''

The Delaware nodded towards Mary Lou, who still lay motionless by the stump. ''That squaw was thrown beneath the wagon. After the warriors left, she came out.

I followed her now for two suns.

"Why did you place your errer in her?"

Allen Crosstree was speaking through gritted teeth.

"She had wandered here to the place of my meeting." It was a flat statement, and quickly Allen looked around. Nothing stirred. So that's why the buck was talking so freely, he thought. He expects someone to come to his rescue. Allen knew now that he'd have to move quickly. He was undecided about the Delaware—whether to slit him or bind him tight and leave him.

The Delaware seemed to read his thoughts and answered the question for him. Suddenly, the buck's feet shot out and struck Allen full in the face while the Delaware started his high-pitched battle cry. It was stopped mid-way as the knife slid home just under the rib cage. The Delaware slowly leaned backwards, his song of death came forth. "Alo may hee—alo may hee!" "I've died a warrior . . . I've died a warrior." And so he died as Ho-Ta-Wa screamed his own Kickapoo death cry. Then suddenly Ho-Ta-Wa jumped towards Mary Lou, who lay terror stricken at what she had witnessed. He snatched her to his breast while running, for he knew the death scream had been heard.

Chapter 4

The fort lay on the east bank of the Saint Mary's and at first glance in the early morning ground fog it gave off the appearance of being deserted. The log gates were closed and no noise or movement could be heard or seen except the ring of an axe indicating that the stockade army cooks were up and making preparations for breakfast.

The Indian scout eased himself as near the log gates as possible, signaling to the braves behind to move forward, but instantly they all stood as if frozen as the tower sentry reported to the Corporal of the Guard. "Post number one, all secure. No sign of man nor beast." The post number two responded until all the corner parapet guards had reported.

One lone figure stepped to the inside stockade gate latch and gently lifted the long bar, while the Sergeant spoke to the guard above, momentarily diverting his attention away from the gate. The one who had lifted the bar silently made his way back towards the officer's quarters, passing the stockade bugler on his way to sound reveille.

It was almost four days since Crosstree had left the fort and General Wayne, now almost completely recovered from the fever, was fully dressed and had been since the middle of the night. He'd been awakened as General Wilkerson prepared to lead a troop of ten dragoons on a scouting party. General Wayne had argued against such a move, but Wilkerson's argument was strong.

"If, General, what this Crosstree says is true, then we need to locate the Injun war party before they reach the stockade. I'll scout out a few thousands rods and if I encounter redskins, then I can warn the post."

General Wayne finally agreed, ordering Wilkerson to be back by one hour after reveille. "Mind you, General Wilkerson, we will need every man we can arm if the Injuns attack. So you get the hell back here!"

"Yes, Sir, General. We'll come a'runnin'!"

Anothny Wayne had stayed up after his scouting party had left under cover of the fog-shrouded night. He was nervous and as he drank the strong tea, he carefully looked at his military map of the Northwest Territory. Recent messages from Fort Dearborn and Forts at the lakes above indicated the major tribes had moved towards Fort Miami. "Damn," he exclaimed, as he studied the new markings he'd made on the map after the latest reports.

He wondered if Hugh Applegate had gotten through. It was doubtful that there would be time, even if he had. That would mean no relief column would be coming. If there was an attack, the fort would have to defend itself. The over-crowded conditions due to the settlers coming in made the situation near to impossible, but the General had felt it necessary to bring them in. He judged the situation too dangerous to leave them undefended.

General Wayne looked out of his window. It was almost first light and his nervous tension was growing. Suddenly, he turned and shouted. "Lieutenant! Lieutenant Price! Come in here!"

The door opened and Sergeant Collins entered,

pulling up his galluses. "Yes, Sir, General. What can I do for you?"

General Wayne frowned. "I want Price. Where the hell is Price!"

"Sorry, Sir, but Lieutenant Price and Sergeant Loomis are gone. They left right after General Wilkerson left on patrol."

"Gone?" the General shouted. "What the hell do you mean—*gone*?"

"Well, General, all I know is Price . . . . I mean Lieutenant Price said Wilkerson had ordered them to scout west of here. Is there somethin' wrong, General?"

General Wayne threw his coffee mug against the wall. The Sergeant jumped. "Damn right, somethin's wrong! Sergeant, tell the guard to double—quick! Have the bugler sound assembly."

The bugler's already on parade, Sir. He . . . ."

The scream filled the entire stockade as the gates flew open and Indians in full war paint charged towards the barracks. The bugler died instantly as the arrow pierced his throat, the note of the bugle dying to a low-pitched gurgle.

"Geesus . . . Saints!" The Sergeant screamed. "Injuns! General, it's Injuns!" But the words fell on deaf ears. General Wayne had already gained the porch, the punk lighter in his hand as he approached the five pounder loaded with grape shot and aimed at the stockade gate.

The cannon's fire spread had momentarily emptied the mouth of the stockade gates, giving Wayne's men time to close the gates and mount a reasonable defense position. But by now, fire arrows had begun to rain into the dry log buildings. As women and children rushed with buckets of water to douse the flames, other fires would start.

The Indians who had gained the stockade had all been killed, but many soldiers and settlers also lay wounded or dead. Colonel Armstrong and his men desperately fought from the stockade parapets. General Wayne had the five pounder moved to the gates to defend against another seige there.

Indians with long pine poles attempted to make a running leap and climb the walls, and some succeeded. As Wayne watched, the parapets became a tangle of bodies slashing and grappling with one another.

The seige continued as the sun rose in the sky, and there were times during the day that the Indians seemed to be gaining the advantage, but the soldiers fought with amazing fierceness, and were able to fend off wave after wave of Indians.

By mid-afternoon, there was a pause in the fighting and the exhausted soldiers slumped to rest as they maintained careful watch.

General Wayne took advantage of the pause to gather his officers to discuss the situation. His worry and the after effects of the fever made him seem like a crazy man as he spoke, and it was clear where the name "Mad" Anthony had come from.

"Colonel Armstrong, who the hell ordered these gates opened this morning? If I find out who did this, I'll have him shot!"

"Don't know, General. Wasn't none of the cook's helpers. The wood was brought in yesterday. Someone said they saw Lieutenant Price on the parade grounds just before they saw the bugler take the arrow, and Corporal Olsen said that Sergeant Loomis was talkin' to the gate sentry just before the attack."

General Wayne cursed. "Price and Loomis! Hell,

they left late last night on patrol. That idiot Wilkerson ordered them out on scout. Sergeant Collins, didn't you say they left right after Wilkerson did?"

"Yes, Sir, General. At least, I thought they did. They was both drawin' supplies when I heard Lieutenant Price tell the supply Sergeant where they was goin'."

General Wayne cursed again. "Wait'll I get my hands on both of them!" He stomped over to the map.

Colonel Armstrong, how many men do we have that can fight?"

"Well, Sir, about one hundred-fifty, countin' some of the settlers. But we're low on powder and shot, General. Our only hope is if Applegate gets through and that would take five days for a draggons unit. Right off, General, I'd say our chances are slim."

Lieutenant Rogers spoke up. "Excuse me, General, but what's wrong with loadin' these wagons and makin' a run down the trace. Seems to me...."

The General interrupted. "Colonel, what's our chances of makin' Cincytown? Has anyone heard from Wilkerson?"

Colonel Armstrong coughed. "General, I wouldn't count on General Wilkerson."

"What do you mean by that, Colonel?" The General scowled as he asked the question.

"Just that if he got caught in that war party, Sir, there isn't a chance in a million that he made it. As for our gettin' out, Rogers might be right. We could make a runnin' fight a lot easier than we could defend here."

Thoughtfully, General Wayne ran his finger down the trace map. Then he turned, pointing to the young Lieutenant.

"What's your name again, Son?"

"Rogers, Sir. Lieutenant Rogers." The Lieutenant

blushed a little.

"All right, Lieutenant Rogers. Arm your wagons and get all them settlers inside, at least the women and children. Make sure there's plenty of water and line them wagons up facing the gate. Colonel, have your men saddle their horses and hold them at the ready."

The General looked at his chronometer. "We probably will get another charge before long. Then let's make a run for it. Colonel, any idea how many Injuns out there?"

Colonel Armstrong shook his head. "Well, cain't rightly tell, General Wayne, but we've already seen three different tribes. Mainly, though, they're Miamis and Shawnee and a few Kickapoo—at least five hundred is my guess."

The charge came at around four o'clock. It would be the last until sunrise. The Indian reasoning was that if a brave died in darkness his spirit could not find its way to the happy hunting grounds. But the enemy attack was a strong one.

Braves had scaled the back wall and those in the stables had a hard time defending that area. The wagons that Lieutenant Rogers had made ready were on fire and as women and children attempted to put the fires out, they fell victim to the constant rain of arrows.

General Wayne had been marked across the forehead with a glancing arrow and as he manned the parapets with his men he was a fearsome sight. The men fought gallantly, but the General knew that it was time to make a break for it. He signaled Rogers to get ready.

As he prepared to leave the wall, a figure off at the edge of the forest caught his attention. "Hell! Look there, Sergeant! It's Little Turtle himself, the chief of the Miamis!"

The Chief rode his Indian pony out into clear view, a defiance in his attitude causing the General to curse. Little Turtle drove his war totem into the ground, his signal that no quarter would be given. Then, to show his total disregard for the American, he carefully draped a 1st Dragoon tunic over the war spear shaft.

"Good God, it's the coat of one of Wilkerson's men," declared Colonel Armstrong to General Wayne.

"Yes, by God. Yes it is, Colonel."

"So General Wilkerson's been caught by the war party. I guess, General, I have to admit that I doubted the General could make it!"

"Me too, Colonel. Me, too." General Wayne seemed sincerely remorseful.

The "run" as it was aptly termed, started immediately after Chief Little Turtle's act of defiance had ended. The warriors had withdrawn to await tomorrow's dawn. Had they know conditions inside the stockade, one more hour of attack would have been sufficient. As it was, they elected to wait for dawn and that wait gave General Wayne and his people the needed time.

Lieutenant Rogers armed every available person inside the wagons and then stationed the outriders alongside. The five pounder was placed on the tail gate of the last wagon with four dragoons inside the wagon to load powder and shot. The Lieutenant reported to General Wayne as he came down from the parapet, saluting smartly as he edged his horse alongside the General's.

"General, I guess we're as ready as we'll ever be."

"Thank you, Lieutenant Rogers. On my signal. . ."

"Yes. Whenever you're ready. We best get movin', though, beggin' the General's pardon."

"You're right, Lieutenant. Return to the wagons."

General Wayne rose in the saddle and surveyed the stockade. "One whole year," he thought. "One whole year with nothin' but smoke to show for it." As he surveyed the scene, he spoke aloud. "I'll be back, Little Turtle. I'll be back."

"What's that, General?" It was Colonel Armstrong broaching the question.

"Nothing, Colonel, nothing." General Mad Anthony Wayne raised his hand for the signal.

Wagons lurched and horses strained in agony as musket fire poured from the wagons into the Indians on each side of the trace. They had successfully caught the Indians by surprise with their strategy, and gained precious time. When an arrow would find its mark into a driver of a wagon, the outriding horseman would come alongside, jump into the wagon seat and take up the reins, some of the dead being shoved off the seat to fall beneath the wagon wheels. Dragoons and cavalry alike fought with musket and saber, driving the Indians into the brush.

Gallantly, Lieutenant Rogers fought from horseback, fighting hard even after taking an arrow in his thigh. As night began to fall, the wagons began to gain their freedom from the Indian band as General Wayne continued leading the run, firing is pistol and reloading at a furious pace.

Wagons crashed into trees and brush as harness rigs were cut or horses fell from arrow wounds and those inside had to be left to fight alone and eventually die.

The Indians suddenly broke off the running battle as darkness settled over the wagons loaded with the screaming and dying. General Wayne surveyed the scene with sadness, tears streaming down his face, as the bodies of women and children and soldiers alike were removed for burial.

The rag-tag- group of soldiers and settlers arrived at Greenville's Crossing badly in need of rest and aid. The wagons carried thirty injured and many families who had been broken up by death over the last few days.

The soldiers from Cincytown who met them were saddened by the sight. After most had been made reasonably comfortable and the wounded had been carried to temporary aid stations, a young man in a neatly starched uniform approached the General.

"Colonel Matthews," he said, saluting smartly.

"Yes, Colonel, what is it?" As General Wayne spoke, he rubbed blackened hands over his eyes.

"Looks like you've made it, Sir." The Colonel's voice cracked with emotion.

General Wayne smiled a feeble smile. "Yes, Colonel, we did. But at a terrible price, I'm afraid."

The Colonel only nodded.

"General Wayne, Sir?"

"Yes, Colonel." He now noticed that the markings on the Colonel's uniform indicated that he was from the military Chief of Staff's office.

The Colonel hesitated. "All right, Colonel. Speak up. What is it!"

"Sir, with respects from the Secretary of the Army, Sir. You are to remain in your quarters. I am to inform you that you are under house arrest."

"What? What the blazes are you talkin' about?" The General could he heared clear across the field. "Arrest? *What* arrest?" Many turned and stared as the General yelled.

"I'm very sorry Sir. Here. This will explain it all. Please, Sir. Go to your quarters. The Secretary will see you when we get to Cincytown." The Colonel handed General Wayne a paper. Across the top in bold type were the words, "TO ANSWER CHARGES."

"Who brought these charges, young man?" The General asked in fury.

"Lieutenant General Mark Wilkerson, Sir."

The General shook his head, his shoulders sagging. He suddenly grew old and tired looking as he read the paper, and the color drained from his face. Without a word he entered the field tent and pulled the flap closed.

Chapter 5

Hugh Applegate stood absolutely rigid. What he saw caused his hair to bristle. He gripped the war belt tightly and gritted his teeth. On the trail ahead some thirty or forty Miami braves trotted in the direction of Fort Miami and the vermillion paint told the story. They were laughing and pointing to one huge warrior who was waving the blond scalp of a woman's hair on one hand while the other, the body of a small baby was being twirled. Overhead, the small corpse was totally mutilated from being struck against the trees.

"Ceerist almighty," Hugh whispered. "Crosstree's friends, no doubt." The old scout's stomach turned at the scene before him. Then two warriors came into view half-carrying, half-dragging a white boy of about ten years. The boy was bleeding about the face and Hugh could see he had no footwear. Occasionally, one of the warriors would strike the boy over the head with his bow and the cracking sound rang out in the trees.

Two of the warriors had stopped on the trail and Hugh made out they were talking about Fort Miami. Hugh listened intently. One of them was a buck Hugh remembered seeing at a rendezvous three years back.

"We are to be given much land by the black bears—land that was ours before, but Little Turtle says we will later kill the black beards as well. I myself will take many scalps on tomorrow's sun."

The other warrior screamed approval, then spoke. "And I, Little Bear, will hang this young white eyes by his heels on the gates. Look at him! Already he faints. A Miami man child would still be fighting." The larger warrior stepped forward and struck the boy a stinging blow. Hugh Applegate's hand went to the hilt of his Pitt steel, but he held still, watching and listening.

Little Bear laughed. "Our women will sing our Songs of Bravery in the lodges this winter."

"Yes," the larger warrior replied. "Come, let us drink whiskey. We can easily overcome the others." He brought forth a clay jug from beneath his quilted blanket.

The column of Miamis was now far ahead as Hugh Applegate lay watching the two warriors with the white boy. His thoughts were on Fort Miami. General Wayne's men would be routed and surely the fort would fall. As he pondered the problem he became convinced that to deliver the belt to Fort Pitt would be useless. It was two, maybe three days away hard running and many painted braves between. It would be too late. Best that he try to save the boy. He thought of Ho-Ta-Wa and how he had started running at the mention of Hayrake's story of the Coogan train.

Hugh remained where he was, even though each time the two Indians struck the litle boy his anger rose. But Hugh had been on the frontier for sixty-three years, having been at Detroit as far back as 1721 with the original Canucks. Patience was his asset and he waited and listened. Little Bear was speaking.

"The braves we found. Did you notice the mark of Ho-Ta-Wa? He is somewhere in these woods right now. I hear he is the captive son of An-To-Wee, the Kickapoo warrior chief."

"Yes, but the chief swears vengence. I heard the medicine man say that Ho-Ta-Wa killed the chief's cousin when he fled the village. Now the Chief says he will burn his white son at the stake when he catches him."

Hugh Applegate smiled. "So ole Ho-Ta-Wa's been real busy," he thought.

As the other buck laughed, Hugh could clearly hear his remark. "It will take many braves to catch 'Silent Wind.' It is said that he is as the ghost. Even the bear Coogan fears his name."

Little Bear sneered. "He is but a white eyes. I myself would kill him without fear." The little boy spoke up. "You aint't fit enought to carry Mister Crosstree's . . . Ho-Ta-Wa's long gun, and he's gonna kill you, you slimy Injuns!"

Little Bear sprang up, drawing his bow and locking in an arrow, but the Pitt steel sank hasp deep in his neck. A moment later, the old Flintlock spoke once and true. The second brave fell face-first, his head striking and breaking the whiskey pot.

Hugh ran like a young boy, sprinting onto the trail. Aaron Sullivan stood wide-eyed, staring at the two dead Indians, then at the running old frontiersman.

"Come on, boy. Let's skedaddle outta here. Won't be two shakes of a hound's tail this here trail be full of redskins. They don't take lightly to such doin's." Hugh grabbed the boy's arm and they broke off into a hickory grove at a fast trot. In the background, Hugh could hear war whoops. It was gonna be almighty close.

The creek was deep and as the sound of whooping and hollering Indians grew closer, Hugh and the boy Aaron crawled in under a mud bank just at the water line of one of the deep holes. Aaron was shivering, but Hugh

Applegate's calmness seemed to have a quieting effect. Aaron lay perfectly still while ripples of water washed across their faces, indicating that the warriors had entered the creek, searching.

Lieutenant Price traveled the trace to the place of his meeting at the sassafras grove. He and his Sergeant had been delayed by warriors going towards Fort Miami and although they were supposed to be friendly, Price wasn't taking any chances.

At the sight of the burned-out wagon train, the Lieutenant threw up as he watched the bottle flies crawl in and out of the eye sockets of Abe Martin. His Sergeant turned away.

"Holy God, Lieutenant. Let's get the hell outta here. Gives a man the creeps. I'm sure glad we're on the right side of those Injuns."

"Me, too, Sergeant. Let's get moving."

The two remounted their horses and rode out at a gallop, still fighting their nausea. It was some time later that the two horses slowed and the Lieutenant indicated an area off to the right of the main trail.

"The grove's right ahead about a half mile. As soon as we meet that Delaware, we'll get back to the Fort."

"What about the Delaware, Lieutenant? Ain't we takin' a chance meetin' him out here? Hell, we both know that if them Miamis or Kicks catch a Delaware this far west they'll be hell to pay."

"Sergeant, ain't you got no sense? We'll kill him as soon as I get that dispatch. We sure don't want Little Turtle findin' out a deal was made with another tribe. you'll take care of it, Sergeant Loomis?"

"Yes, Sir, Lieutenant. Leave it to me."

The two men moved forward cautiously in the

direction of the sassafras grove after carefully hiding their horses. They found the dead Delaware lying just as Allen had left him.

"Damn it! Someone's got here before us. Come on. Let's get out of here," the Lieutenant said. "This place is crawling with Indians."

"But Lieutenant. What about that dispatch. General Wilkerson's gonna be might put out if we don't find that." A quick search revealed that the dispatch was missing. The Lieutenant was becoming extremely nervous.

"Wonder who could have been here? Ain't no sign of Miami or Kickapoo," the Sergeant said.

"I don't know, Sergeant, but we better get the hell outta here. It's a cinch we're gonna be in a lot of trouble if we get back to the fort without it. Let's head east. Then we can cut south into Greenville's place. We can tell 'em we escaped the attack to get help and you keep your damn mouth shut, you hear?"

"Yes Sir, Lieutenant. Lead off." The Sergeant paused and then spoke again. "Ain't that breed Crosstree down this way? I saw him high-tailin' it out from the fort a few days ago."

"Don't worry about Crosstree. He don't know nothin'. Even if he did, don't make no difference. Them two Miamis took care of that. Let's move out. We ain't got a chance on the trace. We'll go east." As the Lieutenant led the way, Sergeant Willie Loomis was sweating, even though a cool breeze was blowing.

Allen was hard-pressed to keep going. Mary Lou's wound had started bleeding and although he had detected no one following them, he was being very careful to leave a difficult trail.

He knew that they were somewhere between Fort Miami and the war villages of the Miamis. More than once, he was forced to take cover while warriors passed by, heading west towards the fort. By their movement it was obvious that the time of the attack had come, perhaps was already happening. The war villages would be practically empty. But Mary Lou was in a bad way. There was no place to leave her. She'd have to travel.

"Mrs. Sullivan, can you keep a'goin'? We're in a bad fix out here. We've got to get further east."

Mary Lou only nodded. She had lost a lot of blood and had no rest. They had been on the run most of the afternoon except the times when Allen threw her under logs or bushes while groups of painted Indians passed by.

"What's happenin', Mister Crosstree? Where are we? Where are we going?" The plea in her voice made Allen stop. He knew he'd have to tell her sooner or later about the attack on the fort and about her children.

"Ma'am, we's somewhere east of Fort Miami. Them braves is dressed out in war paint and feathers. They's headed for the fort to attack it!"

"Fort Miami? What about my younguns! I want to know about my babies." She was crying now. "I don't believe you about Fort Miami, either. General Wayne's there with the army. I'm not going another step until you give me some answers, Mister Crosstree."

Allen seemed frustrated as he spoke. "Ma'am, I ain't got no choice but to take you with me—that is if'n you care about that boy of your'n."

Mary Lou looked shocked. "What about Aaron. Where is he?"

"He's been taken by the . . ."

"My God! Oh my God!! No. Not Aaron." Mary Lou

began to sob.

"Now listen to me. He's alright. At least for now. He's being held at a war village over east of here."

"How do you know that?"

"That brave back yonder told me. He was a Delaware scout. He saw the whole raid on your wagons. I'm right sorry I didn't travel with you folks, but somehow we'll find your boy."

"What about Danielle. Oh God. Don't tell me Danielle's dead?"

"No ma'am. She was taken, too, but by the Kickapoos. They won't harm her—least ways not right now. They're all too busy with the Fort. First, we gotta get to your boy. Then when I got you and him safe I'll go after your girl." Allen didn't tell her that he hadn't figured out how.

"Mister Crosstree, I see I have to go with you, but I'll swear I'll not travel with those horrible scalps hangin' there from your belt any more. You're all covered with blood, and I saw you kill that Indian back there. What *are* you? A savage just like those Indians?"

Allen was momentarily speechless.

"Now don't misunderstand me, Sir. I owe you my life, twice now, and I'm much beholdin' to you. I guess it isn't rightly my business what you do, but for the life of me I can't imagine what you could want with those Indian scalps!"

Allen bristled, and there was anger in his tone. "Look, Ma'am, I didn't have no choice but to kill that Injun back there. He'd of killed me and you, too, if I hadn't a'gotten him first. The scalps, Ma'am, that's the Indian way. When you kill a man you take his scalp."

"The Indian way! Mister Crosstree you oughta be right ashamed of yourself takin' those scalps—even though they are savages. Aren't you a Christian man, Sir?"

"They's no more savages than you an' me, Mrs. Sullivan! Them 'savages' raised me and treated me like one of 'em, but I've seen a few things I reckon you ain't. I was no bigger'n your Aaron when I saw my father skinned alive and then scalped by a bunch of drunken Indians. Nobody was left alive in the whole fort but me. It's people like Jim Coogan makes crazy bucks out of 'em. They's a price on my head ever since I left the tribe and I'd have been dead long ago if I didn't catch them first."

The color had left Mary Lou's face as she stared at Allen. "Your father—skinned and scalped? Oh, Mister Crosstree, how horrible. How did you make it?"

"Luck I guess. Luck and some Injuns that was kind to me . . . some whites, too. I guess you could say I've had more'n my share of luck."

"I can't say I agree with that, Sir," May Lou responded. "But still, could you take those awful scalps away? You haven't any use for them out here in our situation." Her brown eyes pleaded with a soft, warm glow.

Allen still felt a little angry as he took the scalps from the belt and threw them into the bushes. Their eyes met in an uneasy truce.

"I need to bandage that shoulder again, Ma'am. It's bleedin' a mite."

"Alright, Mister Crosstree. I'll be quiet while you do that."

He carefully dressed her shoulder and bound it tight with some of the petticoat she'd torn off for him to use.

"Can you travel now?" Allen asked. "We've got to move afore nightfall."

"Yes, I can travel. Please, Mister Crosstree . . ."

"Allen, Ma'am. Just Allen."

"All right, Allen. I know I'm not strong because of this wound and you must get to Aaron. If I can't keep up, I want you to go on ahead."

"No, Ma'am. Now don't you fret. We'll work it out. Gonna take some doin' but we'll work it out." He eyed her dress. It was snagged and ripped. "Ma'am. Can I make a suggestion?"

"Yes."

"Well. . . ." he seemed embarrassed. "Well, Ma'am. I got two pair o'drawers on and it seems to me you could travel better with buckskins. Why don't I jest slip behind that there bush and shuck one pair and you put 'em on."

There was a merry twinkle in Mary Lou's eye, in spite of her weakened condition. "Well, Mister Crosstree, get to shuckin'."

Soon they were ready to travel again. As Allen looked back at her, he smiled and she smiled back.

They found the village the next day, nestled between two hills. The war lodges showed little sign of anyone being about and it was quiet there. Allen lay on the ridge watching while squaws tended the fires. There was no sign of Aaron and Allen grew worried.

Allen took some time to make a moss bed for Mary Lou under a downed oak. He carried his power horn full of water for her, and made the place far in under the log—being careful to leave a small tunnel so that she would be comfortable.

"You'll be right cozy here now. Whatever happens, don't come out—least ways during the day."

"But where will you be, Allen? Will you be long?" There was fright in her voice.

"Don't expect to be, but fellar can't tell. There's some whoopin' and hollerin' down at the village just now, hear it?"

Mary Lou nodded.

"I ain't seed hide nor hair of Aaron yet. Reckon I'll have to work my way down there for a closer look. If'n I ain't back by sundown tomorrow, you wait until dark. Then head due south. This here ridge comes out sommers of Greenville's place. Hide out and wait. Someone'll come by."

"Please, Ailen. Don't go down there alone. It's too risky. Can't you go for help?"

"There ain't none, Ma'am not now. We's the only whites this side of hell. Excuse me, Ma'am."

"Be careful. *Please* be careful. If anything's happened to Aaron and Danielle, I just don't know what I'll do." She started to cry softly, her shoulders slumping forward. She looked very small and forelorn, like a little girl, and Allen's heart softened. He moved near her and cradled her in his arms, and she slowly relaxed in his embrace, grateful for the comfort.

"You need to rest now, Ma'am," he said, after she had stopped crying. "You're mighty tired. Now crawl in there where you'll be safe and warm. I'll be back when I can."

"Alright, Allen."

She crawled back into the moss under the logs until she was hidden from view.

"Goodbye now, Ma'am."

"Mister . . . . Allen!" she called.

"Yes."

"Take care for yourself, too."

Silently, he was gone.

Mary Lou snuggled into the warm moss. It felt so

good to lay her aching body down, and in a few minutes her exhaustion took over.

Allen could see braves dancing about the fire and the whiskey pots passing steady. He wasn't close enough to hear, but he knew that the assault on Fort Miami must be going well by all the excitement. He wanted to get closer, but as sentries kept cropping up, he had to crawl out of sight. Occasionally an owl hoot would pass along the ridge. That would be the sentries signaling that all was well. Eventually he had crawled a far piece down the ridge. Here he could see more bucks coming in off the war trail. There was much yelling and whopping for they had two soldiers prisoner. Allen couldn't make out who they were but he could see the dragoon blazers well enough to know that they were Fort Miami garrison.

He whispered to himself, a habit of being long in the woods alone. "Those two soldier boys is gonna catch holy ned by them braves. They's tasted blood and victory. Won't be no stoppin' them now." He decided to get closer by crawling into the pole corral where the ponies were kept. Very seldom did Miamis use horses. They kept them for pulling the travis and to load their trade. Usually, the ponies were quite docile. Allen hoped this bunch was as he crept beneath their bellies, trying to gain several fallen trees. There he'd be able to see the entire camp clearly.

He knew that if Aaron Sullivan was being held at the village he would soon be drug out to witness the torturing of the two soldiers and there was no doubt they were going to be tortured. A large log was already buried upright and the squaws had begun to pick up small twigs, laying them in a ring around the base. They were cackling and making obscene gestures towards one of the teepees, but Allen could not see clearly. Then there was a sudden very loud war whoop from the braves as their chief, Little Turtle, came forth from the war lodge. Allen whistled under his breath. "So there's the famous Little Turtle."

Little Turtle was short compared to the other braves, but he was superbly built. Wide shoulders lay beneath a pure otter robe laced with eagle feathers along its edge. As the Chief turned, Allen could see the perfect beaded turtle on the back. The Chief continued to turn in a circle to survey the entire village. The full length of the war bonet lay in a waterfall cascade down the chief's back and trailed on the ground several feet. The feathers had been worked into very small turtle shells that had been polished to a high luster. Allen stared in awe at the imposing chief of the Miamis.

During all the shouting and whooping, the two soldiers were being brought to the stake. They had been stripped naked and as they approached the stake before Chief Little Turtle the largest one began to struggle. There was no mistaking the long blond hair of Lieutenant Price of the First Dragoons. Allen's lips clamped shut. "So Little Turtle ain't got no idea of keepin' his agreement. Else the Lieutenant wouldn't be here," he thought.

As the Lieutenant struggled, a squaw swiftly darted in between the braves and struck the Lieutenant a sounding blow on the testicles with a hardwood stick. The Lieutenant screamed as the squaws danced about and giggled. The blond-haired Price was about to die hard.

The Sergeant was a different breed of cat, Allen thought, as he watched the Sergeant tied to the log while the squaws punched at his privates with sticks. Only once did he cry out and that's when a squaw stuck a sharp stick in his eye. The Sergeant rained curses on the Indians and screamed at the Lieutenant. "You're a sniveling coward, Price! I hope you and your General Wilkerson both pay!" As the flames and smoke began to billow up around the Sergeant's torso, Allen could see Lieutenant Price on his knees before Little Turtle, beggin for his life.

Allen watched for several hours until the Lieutenant died running the gauntlet. By then he knew for certain that Aaron was not in the camp. Where could he be? The brave had said that they had gone east. Was there another camp someplace else?" Allen's exhaustion added to his confusion. Soon it would be dark and he had to make a decision. He couldn't leave the boy. Allen knew that Mary Lou shouldn't be traveling, but what would he do with her? It was while Allen was studying his dilemma that the braves came in from the west, carrying their dead. Squaws begin beating the corpses of the two soldiers as they wailed for the two dead braves now lying at Little Turtle's feet.

A deadly quiet lay over the war village as Chief Little Turtle raised his arms. "It is Little Bear, my only son. See, he is dead by the knife of the white man." Allen could hear every word. The chief continued. "Tell me, did he die bravely at the Fort called Miami?" Little Turtle pointed to the warrior who had carried Little Bear into camp.

"We do not know, great Chief. We found his body with that of the Fox. They had been slain just beyond the white man's road. The Fox had found the white man's metal spear."

Little Turtle stepped forward, striking a sharp blow to the brave who had spoken. "You speak lies! My son died in battle! Cut this liar's tongue out!" Two braves stepped forward, knives drawn.

"Wait!" A voice sounded from the throng of bucks and a tall, lean Indian stepped forward. "Wait!" he repeated. Allen quickly placed his hand over his mouth to keep from sounding out a war whoop as he and Blue Jay used to do as kids while playing in the Kickapoo village. Allen stared in disbelief. It was Blue Jay. After ten years, here before him stood his past in the Kickapoo villages.

Chapter 6

He had been called "Boy" in his first year of captivity, and at the age of ten, true to the tradition of the Kickapoo, Blue Jay's family had decided to adopt him. An-To-Wee was a sub-chief then and considered a great warrior after he had been on a raiding party against the Cheyenne far across the great river to the west. Upon his return, he had been given the privelege of choosing five horses from the village string plus his choice of any two captives. One of his choices had been Allen.

After the death of his father and brother, little Allen Crosstree had made his way down the Cumberland where the Delaware, who fished the falls, found him. Since the tribes were not at war, he was treated fairly well, being traded and exchanged between tribes until a Kickapoo raiding party had taken him from a Sauk village. Though the times were hard in the Kickapoo village, Allen managed quite well. He ate at the fires of many and slept with the village curs.

Blue Jay was the same age and before long the white eyes man child and the son of An-To-Wee became friends. Blue Jay had interceded in Allen's favor and his father completed the adoption.

The summers were lazy and fun-filled for Allen and his adopted brother, but the winters were cold and vicious, and the Kicks moved often so they could hunt for food. Blue Jay and Allen, by the age of fourteen, were permitted to hunt. Each had become strong, apt hunters and trackers.

The one thorn in the side of all Allen's years with the Kicks had been Rapid Water, a young buck a few years older and the cousin of An-To-Wee. Rapid Water hated all whites and the death of his warrior father at the hands of Boone's men caused him to take his revenge out on Ho-Ta-Wa.

Blue Jay also disliked Rapid Water, and that became much worse when the trouble over Dark Fawn started. She had been pledged in marriage to Rapid Water against her will. All knew that Blue Jay felt the "heart tremors" for her. Blue Jay's one fault, his jealousy became apparent then. It soon became an obsession. So bad the situation that the council ruled Blue Jay "an unwise choice" to take An-To-Wee's place when the great chief should die.

Dark Fawn, true to her respect for tribal custom, accepted Rapid Water and made preparations for her marriage. It would never occur to her to doubt the law, even if it meant sacrificing her own feelings. When Blue Jay became obsessed, she soon turned away even from his friendship. This only increased Blue Jay's anger, and the rage became directed at Dark Fawn as well. Ho-Ta-Wa felt saddened by the events, coming to feel that great grief would someday befall due to Blue Jay's hatred. Often he felt his adopted brother was like a stranger, having become a different person from the boy Ho-Ta-Wa had run and.played with.

Over the years, Allen had seen very few white mean and, as required by village law, he was not to be seen when whites were about. But Allen's white instincts caused him many times to creep near the fires to listen to the white trappers, and there were times his heart

yearned for his father and brother. But a Kickapoo was
not permitted to show these feelings. By age sixteen
Allen Crosstree was now fully Indian, a respected young
warrior and hunter, having gone through the rites of
manhood and excelling above many of the Indian braves
in his strength and skill.

He was nineteen when it happened. He was on a
hunting party with some of his friends. Blue Jay had
come, and Rapid Water. Even some maidens were with
them to help clean the animals they killed. Among them
was Dark Fawn. Allen had become separated from the
others and had come across a white man. His curiosity
made him approach, even though he knew he was
violating the law. The white scout, too, was cautious at
first. Having limited knowledge of the Kickapoo
language, he resorted to the universal Indian sign
language.

"What tribe do you hunt with?" There was a long
pause, as Allen's curiosity increased. The man was of
broad shoulders and his regalia indicated he had been to
many tribes. There was a Shawnee hoop piece around his
neck and laced on his right wrist was an eagle tip, at-
tached to a dried scalp skin, indicating the scalp was
taken by the right hand, a true totem of the Iriquois
Indians. All these signs Allen had been taught by his
Kickapoo teachers.

The frontier scout made the sign again. "What
tribe do you hunt with?'"

"I am a Kickapoo," Allen answered in sign.
Carefully, the white scout studied the buck squatting
before him. He looked young but in spite of the dark,
weathered skin and shaved top-knot, there was
something disturbing about him. His answer came
quickly and in an unusual way. Ho-Ta-Wa had squatted

to defecate, lowering his breech clout to one side as was the custom. His buttocks was white as snow.

"Jumpin' catfish," the man exclaimed. "You be a white one!" He stared in disbelief. "Who air ye, boy? What's you a'doin' in them buck's get-up?"

Ho-Ta-Wa stared as he pulled up his clout. The English language was strange but familiar. He tested his lips. "A . . . A . . . Allen. Allen!" He smiled in triumph. "I be Allen Crosstree!"

The white man rose. He was momentarily stunned. "Crosstree! Crosstree! That name sure seems familiar."

Ho-Ta-Wa began to talk some words in Kicky and some in English and great tears were running down his cheeks.

"Whoa, boy. Whoa up, there. I cain't follow you. Now I got it! Abe Crosstree over at McCoffney's stockade. Lordee me, that was way back in '62, maybe '63. They was all massacreed by the Shawnee. Lordee be. Ben's boy. Why Sonny, everyone thought you'd burned up!" The older man slapped Allen's shoulder, then suddenly hugged him. "Whew! You sure smell a sight!" Then he laughed. "My name's Applegate, son. Hugh Applegate."

Suddenly Ho-Ta-Wa tensed, and Hugh Applegate came alert. Ho-Ta-Wa touched his lips with his finger and crouched at the moment that Rapid Water stepped into the firelight.

Hugh backed up, standing ready for trouble. He detected the hate in Rapid Water's face.

"Ah! Ho-Ta-Wa, I see you have a friend." There was no doubting the slur in Rapid Water's statement.

"Yes. Yes," Ho-Ta-Wa replied. "As you can see, we have made a cooking fire together. Come and eat with us." He stood ready, even though his voice was cordial.

"I do not eat with the white eyes, especially one so smelly. Dogs eat only with dogs!"

Hugh understood enough Kicky to catch the insult, and he grasped his knife. "Now lookee here, you stinkin' vermit. . ." the look in the scout's eyes said what Rapid Water could not understand in English.

Ho-Ta-Wa interrupted. "You are no longer welcomed at this fire," he said sharply to Rapid Water. "Go and eat with the squaws." The returned slur carried its full meaning.

Rapid Water gave his battle cry, at the same time leaping the fire, his tomahawk raised. The hatchet which buried itself in Rapid Water's chest came from behind and to the right. Ho-Ta-Wa and Hugh Applegate both whirled, even as the brave crumpled beside the fire. Blue Jay emerged from the woods.

Ho-Ta-Wa's face showed great relief. "Thank you, brother, for my life," he said in Kickapoo. "This is Hugh Applegate, a man who knows about my paw."

"Your father is An-To-Wee, great Kickapoo warrior," Blue Jay answered with contempt. "What is the meaning of your pow-wow with a white man? You know the law, Silent Wind!"

"He is only a scout, my brother, and means us no harm."

"It is because of your foolishness that I had to kill Rapid Water!" Blue Jay answered.

"Hold on here a minute, Crosstree," Hugh interrupted. The English name sounded good to Ho-Ta-Wa's ears, and he stopped to listen. "Lookee here, boy.," Hugh continued in English. "Ain't no call for the two of you to be a hollerin' at one another. It was this here brave a'lyin' by the fire that started the trouble." The words were strange to Allen's ears and he had to strain for understanding. Finally, he nodded and turned to Blue Jay, speaking in Kick.

"The old man speaks true, Blue Jay. Rapid Water attacked, and you defended my life. We will return now to the village with his body and explain to the Chief."

"No!" Blue Jay was suddenly hostile, a wild look in his eye. "I am in trouble with the Council already, Silent Wind. They will say I only found an excuse to kill him. No! It is your fault, brother, for breaking our laws to meet with a white man. It is you who should tell the council you killed Rapid Water. You are respected and have no trouble on your head."

Allen's eyes had narrowed then, his body tensed with anger. "You are my blooded brother, Blue Jay, and I respect our father An-To-Wee above all men, but I will *lie* for no man. Do not ask it of me. You are a Kickapoo warrior, Blue Jay. Such a thought is unworthy of you!"

Blue Jay carried the look of a trapped animal and at that moment the blade of Blue Jay's skinning knife caught the sun. He had drawn it in a motion so quick that Ho-Ta-Wa barely detected it. Hugh moved closer to the tree where his gun was standing. Allen looked at him sharply and spoke. "Do not interfere! This is between us!" Hugh inched away from old Betsy, fresh respect in his eyes.

Ho-Ta-Wa stood tall before his adopted brother. "How is it we must finish this?" he asked.

Blue Jay glanced at Applegate. "He must go."

Allen, in his limited English, directed Applegate to go to the bank of the river and wait. "If I do not appear, you must cross the river quickly, or else Blue Jay will kill you. He will not cross the river after you. Now go!"

Applegate went to the river and Ho-Ta-Wa faced Blue Jay. "Let us begin!" he said.

"It will be. We will use the stick and blade," Blue Jay stated. Then he broke off a hickory limb about four feet long and, holding it in his left hand, he extended the other end to Allen. Allen grabbed it with his left hand and adjusted his grip. Blue Jay's battle cry rang out, and then the battle cry of Silent Wind broke the stillness of the forest.

The knife sliced keenly across Allen's forearm and he bit his lower lip as the sting of the blade made its furrow to the bone. Blue Jay's eyes never left his as Ho-Ta-Wa felt the warm blood running down into his closed hand. Blue Jay feinted, and Allen pulled at the hickory stick with all his strength, at the same time his knife had shot straight out. He could feel the blade grate against Blue Jay's ribs and for a moment, Blue Jay's eyes glazed. Quickly Allen shoved and the knife went between the ribs. For a long moment, Blue Jay's eyes closed. Then his death song started. He slid to the ground gently as Allen withdrew the long thin blade.

It was done. No longer could he live with the Indians. He was an outcast, guilty of killing his own brother. Without a backward glance, Allen Crosstree went towards the river and his return to the world of the white man.

Allen could hardly believe it was Blue Jay standing there before Little Turtle. As the firelight reflected on his body, Allen could see the mark of his knife made ten years ago. Yes, it was Blue Jay, and now he was speaking to Chief Little Turtle.

"You have no reason to harm your warrior. What he says is true. I was with the war party coming from the siege. Both your dead son and The Fox were found on the trail. I have seen the footprint of the white man child. They were joined by the moccasins of one who is white.

We were not successful in finding the boy or the man."

Little Turtle motioned for Little Bear to be removed. His squaw had already smeared her face with ashes and horse dung as she walked the death circle around the corpse of Little Bear.

"If what you say is true, then it is the same one in the moccasins who sent our two scouts away at Bennett's cabin?"

Blue Jay answered. "No. It is not the same white eyes. The one you seek is also the same one who lifted the scalp lock of the war belt carrier."

Little Turtle seemed skeptical. "How do you know this, Kickapoo?"

"It is true," Blue Jay replied. The one we speak of is Ho-Ta-Wa, a white eyes who lived in our village many years. He left his mark on the belt carrier and the two who were at the fort."

"Damn," thought Allen, as he listened. "Leave it to Blue Jay. If anyone could track me it would be him. But what in blazes is he doin' in a Miami war village?"

There was more palaver, but Allen couldn't hear. The rousing cheers of braves coming in to announce that the white man's fort of logs had fallen overrode the other sounds. They were saying that the man general was at that moment beating a retreat south towards the great river.

Little Turtle immediately exhorted his braves to take up the slaughter anew, ordering them to attack the fleeing white soldiers. Then the camp again grew silent as Chief Little Turtle raised his arms.

"The time has come that we shall once again rule our own lands. We will hunt and fish without interference of the white eyes, and our women and children will be safe."

Allen wondered what the chief was leading up to, and when Little Turtle finally reached his point, Allen realized that the Northwest Territory soon would not be safe for any whites. He began to lay his plans as Little Turtle excited his braves by walking up and tomahawking Lieutenant Jimmy Price's body and the remains of the Sergeant. Then he issued hs decree—a decree that would put the frontier in dread for six long years.

"It is now time for all nations to join together—the Shawnee, the Kickapoo, the Cree, the Sauk and the Potowatomis and all that have villages from the big waters to the north to the broad river in the south and on towards the setting sun. Let all of you of the great tribes go forth to your chiefs, asking this of them and let it be known that the Miamis are ready to war on all whites. Let none live who abuse our land and our people. Hunt them down and Kill! Kill! Kill!!" The uproar of the village was deafening. Allen saw then that many tribal respresentatives stood before Little Turtle. He wondered if Blue Jay's standing in the tribe had improved. His mind was full of new questions, for he was still stunned at the sight of one he had so long thought was dead.

Allen slowly worked his way back up the hillside. Aaron was not in the village. That was evident from Blue Jay's message. Someone had taken him from Little Bear and his companion. Allen thought he knew who that someone was. Now the trick would be to get out of the territory to safety. It was hundreds of miles east to the Monongahali and the safety of Fort Pitt and it was two or three days southeast to Cincytown, with every avenue of escape shut off. Now is the time that Allen wished for help.

Mary Lou did not answer Allen's call at first and panic momentarily rose in his breast. Had some brave stumbled upon her? Or had she left her hiding place? Quickly, he knelt by the deadfall and crawled in. Mary Lou was sitting in a half-crouched position, the skinning knife thrust out before her. There was terror in her eyes. Allen spoke quietly and in a gentle tone. "It's me, Ma'am. Don't be alarmed. Try to move over somewhat. We'll have to hole up here until night." Allen moved in to lie at a prone position next to Mary Lou. There was a faint sweetness to her, mixed with a hotness that told him she was feverish. As he lay there, his shoulder touched hers. He felt his heart racing faster.

There was fear in her question as she whispered. "Did you see Aaron?" Allen thought it best not to cause her any more worry than necessary as he answered. "No ma'am. But there's news of sorts. It peers like someone took him away from two Miami bucks."

"Other Indians?" Mary Lou seemed panicky.

"No, a white man," Allen answered.

"Thank god," she whispered, lying back.

"Well now, that ain't all. Whoever it was killed them bucks and one was. . . ." instantly Allen's hand went over Mary Lou's mouth as he tensed. Someone or something was just over them, climbing on the deadfall. Allen's tomahawk and his knife came to the ready but he knew they would be useless. He was lying down. There would be no room for defense. He could feel Mary Lou trembling as small pieces of dirt cascaded down on them from the added weight above. Allen eased down towards the opening. His thoughts were on Mary Lou. Maybe if he sprang out, they—whoever they were—would think he was alone. It could save her life, providing of course, she could get out of the territory. Allen knew there would be no prisoners now. Little Turtle had sealed the fate of all whites caught—man, woman or child.

Faint voices came from above, peculiar voices, but they were not clear. Something was not right. Allen knew that if the braves were tracking there would be no conversation. If words were needed as they tracked out their quarry, only sign languaged would be used.

Cautiously, he slid lower, his heart pounding against his chest. Mary Lou's hand came to rest on his bicep, then gently but firmly squeezed with a tugging motion indicating her desire for Allen to remain. He reciprocated by laying his hand on hers, but his body tensed for the spring out into the opening from under the giant oak log. There would be only one chance and every muscle in his sinewy body was turned for that final effort.

Chapter 7

Hugh Applegate, in spite of his years, was a remarkably fit man. Stories of his feats on the frontier had long ago become legendary and his actions on the day of his rescue of Aaron Sullivan did much to confirm the tales.

Aaron had survived his three-day capture quite well, in spite of the beatings, and the agility of this nine-year-old surprised even Hugh. From the moment when the two braves fell upon the trail, victims of Hugh's knife and long gun, little Aaron Sullivan had bravely maintained his run gainst death with his companion rescuer.

They had eluded the Indians searching for them in the river by remaining perfectly still until nightfall. Then they had traveled all night, resting only for short periods of time when they felt reasonably safe. Once Hugh even let Aaron stand guard while he caught a quick nap. Few words had been spoken by either during the entire escape—Aaron, due to his fright, and Hugh simply because, as he put it later, "there ain't no use wastin' a fellar's wind."

By afternoon of the next day, Hugh had time to think over their situation. He figured that the main tribal concentration would be south and somewhat east as the warriors traveled to and from their war villages to continue their siege of Fort Miami. He had no plan yet, except to stay away from the Indians. On several occasions, the crusty old scout had to rely upon memory as to trail locations which would not be intersected by the Indians. At one point, they came upon such an intersection and were startled to hear voices on the trail.

"We'd best be takin' cover, boy," Hugh said hurriedly. "It sounds like a war party."

Two large burned-out pine trees lay just off the trail, creating natural hollow logs. It was there that Hugh placed Aaron in one of them while he sought shelter in the other. The two logs offered safety, but at a price. As Hugh plunged into his log, feet first, he felt with his moccasined toe a small animal that turned out to be a polecat with a definite resentment towards the intruder. The odor was overpowering, but the old scout had to lie still and hold his breath, for there, just in front of the log, were the feet of several warriors who had by now also come in contact with the misty essence of the animal. One brave, a Miami, was laughing as he spoke.

"We have come upon one who spits backwards. The smell is terrible. Come, let him have this part of the forest."

One of the companions replied, "Yes, but what caused him to spit? Maybe we should look around. You yourself heard our chief say to the Kickapoo warrior that somewhere in this area two white eyes now escape our braves. One is the dreaded Ho-Ta-Wa, who killed our brothers. The other is the one who struck down The Fox and Little Bear and has taken the white-eyes man child."

The first brave impatiently replied. "I, too, heard these things, but do not look for shadows. The white eyes would not be this close to our war village. Come, let us be gone to the fort. They say that the mad general has broken out with some of his long knives and is at this moment running the white-eyes road to freedom."

The second brave seemed reluctant to leave, and Hugh was getting desperate for air—for the polecat now had started walking up his back towards the open end of the log. Hugh prayed that one of the bucks would not squat to investigate.

The brave who spoke of the fort continued, "Come. We cannot lift the scalp of a skunk. There will be much whiskey at the fort and many things for our squaws. Come!"

At that moment, the skunk politely walked over top of Hugh's head and out the end of the log. It was then that the warriors decided it best to leave, and Hugh sucked in fresh air.

The old scout remained in his misery for quite some time, making certain that all was safe before crawling out of the polecat's home into fresh air. Then he crawled to the smaller log to extract Aaron.

"Whew-eee, Mister. You sure smell a site!" Aaron grinned while Hugh quickly rubbed himself with milkweed. They rested for several minutes.

"What your name be, boy?"

"I'm Aaron Sullivan, Sir." Then great tears slid down the little boy's soot-streaked face. "My maw and paw was kilt by the Injuns back on the way to Fort Miami. Them savages took me captive. They took my sister, too." For the first time since it all happened, Aaron was crying.

"Hush now, boy. Ain't no time for that. We's in one heck of a predicament and we's need to save all our vitals to get through." The old scout gently placed his right hand on the boy's shoulder as he spoke. "Air you the friend of Ho-Ta-Wa?"

Aaron immediately perked up. "Do you know him? Mister Crostree?"

The old man nodded his head.

"Where is he? If'n he was here, we'd be all right."

"Easy, boy. Easy now. Yep, I reckon your Mister Crosstree and I air right good friends. Why, we's go back plumb to the Cumberland. Why, I taught ole hoss Ho-Ta-Wa everythin' he knows."

"But where is he? Is he at that there fort?"

"Ain't no fort no more, boy. That's what them savages was a palaverin' about. That and that dad-blamed skunk! I don't rightly know where he is, but accordin' to them savages, he's still on the loose. We'd best be gettin' on. Must be a war village sommers east of here. We'll have to be almighty quiet—you hear?"

The old scout thrust a piece of jerky into Aaron's hand. "Chomp on that a spell. It'll cool your innards a mite." The boy gorged the half-raw jerky. It has been four days since he had eaten.

Hugh regarded Aaron as he would a man, for he had witnessed the young boy's sand under stress and he knew he could depend upon him. As Aaron ate, Hugh began his instructions on their future.

"Now as I seet it, we're smack dab in the middle of the biggest Indian uprisin' since '65, and we ain't gonna have no easy time of it gettin' to the outside. That there means, boy, that we is gonna have to skeedaddle into a deep hole until that there daylight dwindles a mite. Best we move at night." As Hugh talked, Aaron nodded complete understanding as his adam's apple bobbed up and down, urging the jerky into his innards. Hugh continued. "Now not far from here is a big oak grove with lots of downfall. We best get over there and dig in. Now you stay close behind me."

"Do I have to, Sir? That smell is right powerful."

"Hush your mouth, boy. A little skunk juice ain't

nothin' like havin' your butt full of Miami errers." Hugh smiled as he led off.

They moved cautiously into the oak grove. Hugh bent double, seeking just the right place. Then he spied a good-sized hole going in under two giant logs. He saw the moccasin tracks as he approached, and he signaled for Aaron to hang back and be quiet. At first he was puzzled. Then, as he bent and studied the prints, a smile creased his leathery face. He signaled for Aaron to start talking. Aaron was surprised, but he knew better than to go against Hugh's instructions. So he did as bidded while the old scout climbed upon the fallen log above the hole, taking up a good-sized limb as he did so. He was chuckling as he stood waiting atop the log, and Aaron was convinced the old man had gone crazy.

The man in buckskins suddenly sprang from the hole, both knife and hatchet thrust out before him. The blow from Hugh's limb sent him reeling forward as it descended across his shoulders. As the man rolled forward, he doubled for the spring that would confront his attacker. What he saw before him made him blink. Then he turned beet red.

Hugh was chuckling without sound, as he stood atop the oak log, the stick held firmly in both hands, while Aaron stood wideeyed, staring at Allen Crosstree.

"Uh-huh! Gottcha, you vermit! Right in your hole," and as Hugh spoke, he spat.

Aaron found his voice and his legs at the same time. "Mister . . . Mister . . . Ho-Ta-Wa! It's you!" The boy ran straight towards Allen's outstretched arms.

Mary Lou emerged from the tunnel as soon as she recognized Aaron's voice. There were tears in her eyes as she ran to him and cradled his head in her arms.

"Why Aaron Sullivan, you're a sight for sore eyes!

What's happened to you, son?"

"I'm all right now, Mama, but I thought you was dead back there! I thought you was dead!" he was laughing and crying at the same time.

"You did this somehow, did't you Allen?" Mary Lou asked, turning her radiant face toward him. "Or is it a miracle?"

"Neither, Ma'am, I reckon," Allen answered. "I told you I was a right lucky feller."

Mary Lou lifted Aaron's face up, releasing him from her smothering embrace. "Are you all right, son?"

"Yes, Mama. This man here. He got me away from the Injuns."

Mary Lou reached her good arm out to the stranger and smiled. "My name's Mary Lou Sullivan, Sir, and I'm mighty grateful to you."

Hugh seemed embarrassed, but he smiled shyly. "Twern't nothin', Ma'am. Name's Hugh Applegate."

"Nothing, Mister Applegate? If those savages still had Aaron he'd . . . . well, no tellin' what would have happened to him." The tears were brimming in her eyes again and the color had left her face. Allen quickly stepped forward and put his arm around her. He was just in time, for she was about to faint.

"We gotta get you off your feet, Mary Lou, and I gotta get that bandage fixed again. This here trail's gonna be filled with drunken Injuns comin' from the fort before long. Hugh, you crawl in under there and make a little more room for these two while I tend to the lady."

As Allen bandaged Mary Lou's shoulder, their eyes met and she smiled. "You're very kind, Allen. Thank you very much for taking care of me."

"I'm glad you've got your boy back," he said. "But you've got some fever and you're gonna have to be quiet and still and give yourself some time to get better. Will you do that?"

"Yes, I'll do that," she said.

He touched her cheek before he helped her up, his grey eyes betraying his feelings.

Hugh had finished the preparations and Allen instructed Aaron and his mother to crawl inside and remain absolutely still. Hugh shared the last of his jerky, then the two scouts sealed the hole, careful to brush out all the tracks. Their decision had been made. Should discovery be made, Allen was to lead the savages off while Hugh doubled back to retrieve his two charges. Then he was to work his way south towards Cincytown on the big river. If all went well, they would all travel after the warriors had gotten good and drunk at the war village.

When all was ready, the two men stood outside and grinned at each other. "Peers, ole hoss, we got ourselves quite a predicament, what with a wounded woman and a wore-out youngun." Hugh jerked his thumb towards the Mother and son as he spoke. "I done heard your name on the trail. Them savages want to talk to you mighty bad about them dead braves."

Allen smiled. "Well, you old crow bait, we's in the same fix. So happens one of them warriors you did up when you rescued the boy was Little Bear, ole Chief Little Turtle's only man child heir. I reckon both our hair ain't none too healthy right about now."

Allen explained all he had heard and seen since he last saw Hugh at the fort, and Hugh told his tale. Then they decided to seek a hiding place so they could watch the trail, and then they settled in. The wait was brief.

Warriors came in pairs, fives, tens, and in several instances in groups of thirty to fifty. It was hard to

88 THE LEGEND OF HO-TA-WA

determine whether they were Kickapoo, Miami or
whatever, due to the moon skirting in and out behind the
clouds, but on two seperate occasions the two frontier
scouts counted Miami, Kicks, and to their amazement,
Shawnee. Every warrior appeared to be drunk and they
carried the bloody clothing of soldiers. Several times the
heads of dead dragoons could be seen stuck to the top of
long poles giving off a grizzly scene that caused the two
scouts to curse beneath their breaths.

One group stopped to drink only a few yards from
the hidden scouts. Their war whoops and screams
subsided and soon the braves sat down upon the trail and
in typical boisterous terms described the fort's fall.

Allen gathered from what he heard that the siege
had actually lasted only some ten hours, at the cost of
over two hundred dragoons under Anthony Wayne's
command. Many of the settlers taken into the stockade
were also killed. He learned of the running battle after
the fort had fallen, also. Silently, he thanked the great
power for steering his moccasins away from the fort with
Mary Lou Sullivan.

At one point, the names of Coogan, General
Wilkerson and Lieutenant Price came up. The braves
revealed that Coogan, suspecting a trap by the Indians,
had made escape along with General Wilkerson. Allen
and Hugh listened carefully to the brave, a Miami by his
language, who spoke.

"We were ordered to kill both Coogan and the white
eyes leader, but somehow they slipped our nets. It is said
that the white leader arranged for the gates of the fort to
be opened to us."

"Yes," replied another. "We knew of his help to us.
But the white leader will soon meet the fate of his blond-
haired sub-chief, who the drums say died as a coward at

the war village. We will all be on the trail tomorrow.
Little Turtle has decreed that both the whiskey peddler
and the General must die.''

Another brave spoke up. "The mad general also
made his escape but I have already counted his coup.''
The rest laughed. Shortly, all gathered their plunder and
proceeded towards the village.

Hugh put his lips to Allen's ear. ''That skunk
Wilkerson got clean away.''

Allen, in turn, repeated the gesture, speaking,
"Yes, I heard. If he gets to Cincytown first, it would
mean trouble for General Wayne. Maybe one of us
should head that away and report what we know.''

"Hell, Hoss. Ain't we all goin' thataway?'' Hugh
asked.

Allen answered with sterness. ''No! There is still the
little girl. She is bein' held at the village of An-To-Wee
and I mean to get her back if'n she's alive.''

"You're plumb loco, hoss. This whole country's a
crawlin' with redskins. Anyway, how you figure to travel
with that sick woman and that tyke. Ole hoss, you gotta
cross clean through Injun country to Kicky land, and I
ain't figurin' that An-To-Wee's gonna be too happy to
see you—or ain't you rememberin' Rapid Water and
that feller Blue Jay?''

Allen made a matter-of-fact statement. ''I ain't
forgot, Hugh. But blame it, that there woman tucked
under that log back yonder with that little boy would
plumb grieve herself to death. Anyways, I might as well
settle this here score between me and the Chief. I seen
Blue Jay back there at the Miami village, ole Hoss.''

"Blue Jay? You mean your Kicky brother? But you
kilt him ten years ago?''

"Guess not. It was him for sure. Still bore the scar

of my knife. He's as alive as you and me, down there a pow-wowin' with Little Turtle.''

Hugh whistled softly through his teeth. "All these years you been a runnin' and twern't no need.''

"Musta been some need, ole Hoss. They's been after me all this time.''

"True. That's true, boy.'' Hugh paused. "So you's wantin' to go back and face your Daddy, 'eh?''

"That's about the size of it. That'n that little girl what belongs to that woman back there.''

"Well, Sonny. I reckon, then, that them that can is them that will. So best we be gettin' about our chore!''

"No, Hugh. I ain't askin' you to tak epart. Seems this be my chore.''

Hugh spat before he placed his lips to Allen's ear. "Ho-Ta-Wa, go plumb to hell. I'm in, anyways. I'm too sceered to make that trip to Cincytown alone.'' He chuckled. Allen turned to face the girzzled old timer. Then, in true Indian fashion, his hand closed upon Hugh Applegate's forearm in the universal arm shake. Allen was grateful.

It was almost dark when Allen and Hugh helped Aaron and Mary Lou crawl from their hiding place. Mary Lou seemed rested and the fever had broken. Her eyes were clear.

"She's better,'' Allen thought, with great relief.

"Well, Ma'am,'' he said. "We's gonna do some more travelin'.''

"Travelin'?'' Mary Lou echoed.

"We's gonna go get your little girl.''

Mary Lou's face showed relief and joy. "Thank you, Mister Crosstree. From the bottom of my heart, I thank you.'' She stood on her tiptoes to kiss his cheek, and he colored. Mary Lou's brown eyes twinkled.

They prepared for their departure hurriedly. They traveled all night, as rapidly as possible, skirting the Miami war village, knowing that at least for the night they were safe. Mary Lou and Aaron did not complain at the grueling pace, and Mary Lou's spirits were high.

Mongo flats lay west and north and Allen knew that country well. Soon, as daylight began to peek through the sycamores, all four were well concealed in an abandoned bear cave. Hugh brought water for both Aaron and his mother in reed tubes and soon the two were sound asleep. Then he and Allen layed out their strategy.

"Ho-Ta-Wa, we's got a mite of ground to cover. Ayr ye certain that the gal's at the Kicky village?"

Allen thought Hugh's question over carefully before answering. He had been thinking of little else for the last two days. The two Miamis he had killed, then the others, Blue Jay's statement back at the war village—they all convinced him that it all had something to do with him. The girl had been deliberately taken to An-To-Wee for some reason and he had been asking himself why. There was one obvious reason. An-To-Wee wanted his adopted son to come to him. And what about Blue Jay? Was he running with the Miamis? There didn't seem to be any other answer.

"Yes, Hugh. I'm certain. She's there, but for one reason—me."

"You! What do you mean—you?"

"I don't know rightly, but it all has somethin' to do with me and the leavin' of the tribe and Rapid Water's death. You been out here since the Frenchies. Ever hear of the Kickys takin' a girl captive?"

Hugh shook his head no.

"Well, then," Allen continued. They knew I was

here. Musta watched me followin' the train. Ole An-To-Wee's smart enough to let the Miamis run me right to him. I ain't never heered of the Kicks goin' to war with any other tribe, neither. They prefer to work the war path alone."

"Me neither, come to think about it," Hugh replied. "Peers ole An-To-Wee wants you mighty bad, son. I'd be mighty careful."

Allen smiled. "Hugh, I have an idea. What's the one thing the Injuns understand?"

Hugh spat. "Well, now. The only thing comes to mind is bravery. Them redskins plumb admire bravery."

Allen laughed. "Rightly so, Hugh. Ole Hoss, they's mighty brave people. I'm a thinkin' I should jest hike right on into that camp and ask ole An-To-Wee for the girl."

"Son, you got lots o' sand. I ain't denyin' that, but you best think this one over. We both know the Kickys is a dyin' tribe. Heck fire, ain't over four hundred braves left, and they ain't likely to think there's much to lose if'n they have a little sport with you. I reckon that'll 'bout do 'em in. So leavin' you behind don't sound like somethin' they'd do. Remember ole Henry Likkens?"

"Yep. Sure do," Allen answered. "Saw Henry at Fort Miami jest 'fore the Kicks caught him for killin' that squaw up on Saint Joe's stream."

"Well, I lay up on that north slope and watched that whole thing. Lordee, that fellar took two days to die. You remember that, son, 'cause I sure would hate to watch you a hangin' over a fire pit." Hugh place his hand on Allen's shoulder.

"Hell, I'm a thinkin' you could take the woman and boy on south," Allen answered. "I'll catch up."

"Isn't no way. . . ." Mary Lou spoke as she walked up, surprising both men. "Allen Crosstree, we're not leavin' you out here alone. I've been hearing you both. Why can't we get the army to come up here and help? It's for sure, though, that we're not leavin' you."

Allen was embarrassed. "Ma'am. . . ."

"Don't you 'Ma'am' me, Allen Crostree, or Ho-Ta-Wa, whatever you're called. We've been through to much to lose anyone else we care for!" Her voice was stern and her meaning clear. Hugh interrupted.

"Now lookee here, you two. We ain't exactly inside a stockade where's you can bicker. Ma'am, pardon my sassiness but there ain't no army. Hells bells. Ole Mad Anthony right now is a high-tailin' it towards Cincytown. He ain't what you might call fittin' fer battle. No Ma'am. This is somethin' we gotta do alone, and Ho-Ta-Wa and me goes together. We can stash this here woman and boy some place safe," he finished, looking at Allen.

Mary Lou was angry. "Now both of you might as well figure on me and my son taggin' along. We've been in this frontier twelve years come fall. So don't concern yourselves that we're not fit. Where you go—we go!

The subject seemed closed.

Allen spoke. "All right, then it's settled. But remember it's got to be to my thinkin' how we'll get into that village. Agreed?" No one replied, but both Hugh and Mary Lou knew Allen's decision was final.

Chapter 8

In the late spring heat, Mongo swamp gave off an eerie appearance. Low fog lay over the water, and the trees were so dense that little sun was allowed through. As the four weary travelers surveyed the area, it was easy for them to see why the Indians were afraid of the place.

"What is this place?" Mary Lou asked. She was whispering, even though there was no need.

"It's a fearsome place to the Injuns," Allen answered. "That's why it's a good place to leave you and your youngun. It is said that the spirit of the wicked old medicine man, Haa-In-Mott, lives here. There's been whole raidin' parties disappeared in this here swamp, and some o'their totems was found hangin' from the mimosa trees. So the Injuns—well, they jest don't come in here no more. It's what they call 'taboo.' "

"Oh my," Mary Lou whispered.

Aaron's eyes were big as saucers. "Will ole Haa-In-Mott get my maw and me if we stays here?" he asked.

"Ain't no way, youngun. He's afeared of little boys, so's I hear. Won't come nowheres near 'em." Allen's eyes twinkled, though his face was solemn, and Mary Lou nodded her thanks to him.

The place where the two Sullivans were to be left was chosen carefully by Allen and Hugh. Allen had long suspected that Mongo Swamp held more than old Haa-In-Mott's ghost, but his years in the village had also instilled in him some respect for the legend. It was apparent he was tense and nervous being there and that leaving Mary Lou and Aaron did not appeal to him.

When Allen went off to get meat, Hugh responded to Mary Lou and Aaron's questions by telling what he knew of Allen's experiences with the Kickapoo and his ten years in the villages.

Mary Lou was sympathetic as she spoke with Hugh. "That man not only saved my life at Cincytown, but gave me and my younguns a will to go on. I . . . we are grateful. Is he married to an Indian, Mister Applegate?" She blushed at her forwardness in asking such a question.

"No, Ma'am," Hugh answered. "He ain't catched. He sure is taken with you and them younguns." Hugh's direct answer caused Mary Lou to blush again.

"You watch over him, Mister Hugh, and bring him back safe."

"Yes, Ma'am. But he's a good scout, so ain't no need to worry yourself. You jest stay put and don't go movin' about. This here place is almighty scary and you cain't never tell when some crazy buck'll come traipsin' around here. Will you do as I say?"

"Yes, we will," Mary Lou answered.

"Now one thing I gotta do is put a poltice on that shoulder."

Mary Lou nodded and Hugh carefully dressed the shoulder, putting a milkweed poltice on it.

"It's a'healin' mighty fine, Ma'am," he said. But Hugh lied. The shoulder was infected and a frown crossed the old scout's face. She'd need attention soon.

Allen returned with a deer and quickly seared some of the meat over a smokeless fire. "It ain't exactly cooked, Ma'am, but it'll keep you and the boy full and the red meat'll do that shoulder a heap of good." Allen's glance at Hugh said what he really meant.

"Thank you, Allen. We'll be just fine. You best be gettin' on. Don't worry none about us." She smiled a wan smile. Allen knew she was tired and feverish. He turned to Aaron.

"All right, boy. You are the chief scout here now. You take real good care of your Mama and don't go traipsin' around. Stay put. And if'n you see any movement down yonder at all, you lay real quiet. Hear?" Allen handed the boy his war hatchet.

Aaron's chest swelled as he accepted the hatchet. "Don't you worry, Ho-Ta-Wa. I'll take good keer of my Maw."

Allen and Hugh back-tracked off the small knoll at the edge of the swamp, carefully wiping out all traces of their coming and going. Then they thoroughly scouted out the area before leaving. It was then they found something that both amazed and confused them—wagon tracks, ending at the edge of the swamp. Allen knelt, examining the tracks while Hugh scouted the area around. When he returned, they spoke, invoking the sign language.

"There have been horses—army horses—no shoes."

Allen responded in sigh. "Yes. And I've found army boot marks mixed with moccasins. Supposed to be no Injuns around here. What do you think?"

Hugh rubbed his face thoughtfully. "Seems somebody's usin' this swamp—somebody who ain't afeared of ole Haa-In-Motts' spirit. But we must go now." The old scout made the motion by rubbing the palms of his hands as he extended his arms outward. Allen replied in like fashion, then he touched his breast with his thumb, meaning "come back." Hugh nodded and the two scouts made for the Kickapoo village.

An-To-Wee's village lay west of Mongo Swamp some thirty leagues and it nestled between two fairly high hills, making access to the village practically impossible unless one wanted to be seen. High on the west hill, pole racks stood in neatly aligned patterns and testified to the tribe's reverence for the dead as indicated by the colorful ribbons, war shields and intricately woven blankets which decorated them. That piece of ground was sacred and reminded all that the tribe was short of braves. The Delaware/Kickapoo wars had taken their toll several years before. History had testified that it was not because the Kicks were losing warriors—quite the contrary. They were fierce battlers, inflicting large losses on their enemies. But their fierceness seemed to be their undoing as well—to the point of suicide in battle. This had resulted in what would eventually lead to the tribe's total extinction.

Allen and Hugh lay on the East hill observing the main village. Each passing moment gave them a sense of growing despair at the prospect of ever being able to penetrate the village undetected. That big things were happening was obvious and two such events infuriated both of the scouts.

An-To-Wee's squaw came from the chief's teepee draggin someone who was tied. They shortly made out that it was the little girl Danielle, and Allen tensed as he witnessed the squaw beating the girl with a switch, while other children and old women stood around and jeered. Allen could hear the little girl's cries, and he raised to a half-crouch. Instantly, Hugh's hand closed on his shoulder. "Easy, ole hoss. Easy. It ain't time yet." Allen eased back.

The little girl's torment ceased as a great uproar came from the valley. A group of braves rode in with Blue Jay at their head. Riding beside him was none other than big Jim Coogan. The braves were throwing soldier's clothing to the squaws. Old men and children were running along side, banging pots and pans that had been taken from the fort, while Coogan and Blue Jay rode towards An-To-Wee's teepee. The chief had emerged, ready to receive his warrior son. Clay jugs full of whiskey were unloaded and the great celebration began.

Hugh and Allen both knew that perimeter scouts would be out, so they cautiously crept to the far end of the valley and crossed over into the sacred burial grounds. Allen shivered as he crawled beneath the burial racks of those he had hunted with for so many years. He was still enough Kickapoo to feel afraid of violating the sacred grounds, but from that vantage point they could at least see and hear.

Jim Coogan was arrogant as he sat between the great chief and Blue Jay during the victory dances. The entire tribe was soon drunk and a great feast was prepared while the chief and his council returned to the council teepee with Coogan. The two scouts now hidden in the sacred burial grounds knew that Coogan was up to something and they were anxious to find out what. Little Danielle had been momentarily forgotten and they could see her lying on a pile of buffalo robes, apparently asleep from exhaustion. The scouts spoke to each other in sign.

"White man is up to no good."

Allen replied, "Why did the Miamis slay the Lieutenant and Sergeant? How did this one get away? Where is Wilkerson? I heard the Miamis say themselves that all would be killed."

Hugh spat before he signed a reply. "Seems that Coogan has some special interest in the Kicks. Some say he has been seen at Dearborn."

Allen's eyes grew slate grey as he signed back. "Then that's it. Coogan has no longer any use for the Miamis. The Kickapoo know Dearborn well. Is he wanting them to attack Dearborn?"

Hugh replied, "Seems likely. Then there would be no American forts to contend with. The black beards could move in." He paused, then continued. "That swamp! It has something to do with the swamp!"

Allen stared at the old scout. He knew Coogan moved among all the tribes and forts and it made sense. Coogan was the black beard agent, and he would use the tribes to war for the advantage of the Spanish.

Allen studied the scene below carefully. It was possible that after dark he could get into the village and rescue Danielle. He could cause a diversion so Hugh could take the girl and escape. In spite of his wait, however, the Kickapoo continued to celebrate during the night by holding races, feats of strength and other games that kept the entire village active. By sunrise, both scouts knew there was no way into the village. Allen's original idea seemed the only way.

There was no use in Hugh's argument, delivered in sign language. Allen's mind was made up. He stripped just to his leggins and breech clout, even as Hugh still argued with him in sign. Allen had found a pot of dye left at one of the grave sites. With his upper torso bare, he carefully used the dye as he had been taught. Upon completion, Allen Crostree now in truth became Ho-Ta-Wa. He made a fearsome sight. Silently, he gave Hugh instructions as he finished preparations. The village below had quieted somewhat, but An-To-Wee and his council, along with Jim Coogan, were still inside the council teepee.

Allen stood, raising both hands, and with arms extended upward, he chanted his victory song in a low key. Hugh stood silent, knowing that Ho-Ta-Wa was about to be tested beyond the imagination. When he had finished his preparations, Hugh stepped close and whispered. "Take care, ole Hoss. That woman back yonder needs you. So's them younguns."

Allen stared. "It is so with me, Hugh Applegate, and tell her so!" Hugh nodded. He would do as Allen asked.

Then Ho-Ta-Wa silently worked his way down the hillside and, in direct line to Danielle, who still lay on the buffalo robes, Ho-Ta-Wa readied himself to enter the village he had not seen for ten years.

Ho-Ta-Wa slowly worked his way parallel to the village until he had reached the furthermost end where Sycamore Creek passed between the hills. When he had reached the mouth, he crossed the creek to a meadow facing the village. Again, he raised his arms, but this time his warrior's call was a loud scream.

The village was instantly electrified. Braves grabbed their bows and spears, running up the village street. Squaws were screaming. Then Allen heard, "Ho-Ta-Wa!"

The name was repeated by others, "Ho-Ta-Wa. Ho-Ta-Wa! Ho-Ta-Wa has returned!" The screams reached An-To-Wee in the council teepee, and he quickly emerged with a commanding presence and called in a loud voice, "Do not kill him!"

Ho-Ta-Wa stood rigid as the village braves rushed towards him, shooting arrows into the ground around him. Stones struck his body, thrown by the squaws and children. As Ho-Ta-Wa watched the village rush towards him, he could see a blurr of movement far down the slope of the sacred burial grounds. Hugh would wait until the right moment. Then he would free Danielle.

An-To-Wee shoved squaws and braves aside as he made his way through the throng to confront his adopted white eyes son. There was rage in his eyes as he stood before Ho-Ta-Wa.

"Ah, so you have come back. Your bravery is well-noted since you have gone from us. Why have you returned now? We have waited long."

Ho-Ta-Wa spoke. "Great Chief An-To-Wee, I have come to ask why my brothers chose to take up the war path against the whites."

An-To-Wee stook a step forward. "You dog dung, we made you one of us and now Rapid Water lies with the skeletons of the hawk while you plotted against us. You are like all whites—forked-tongued and without honor."

Ho-Ta-Wa's face showed amazement. Rapid Water? He was charged with the death of Rapid Water! His mind whirled momentarily, for he realized that he would never have had to leave his tribe if he had come back and told the truth. It was useless to try and respond now, but he determined that if there was any way, he'd avange himself.

A voice from the throng cried out, and Blue Jay stepped forward. "So, Ho-Ta-Wa, you *did* come. We knew you would, but it is for nothing. See? Now we not only have the girl child but your friend as well." Blue Jay signaled and the throng parted, revealing little Danielle held by the hair. Alongside her on his knees was Hugh Applegate, with two braves at his side. One of them held a knife at his throat. The bait had been taken.

Coogan now stood alongside Blue Jay. "Kill them. Kill them! He is a traitor to your people!" Coogan urged.

Ho-Ta-Wa spoke, his voice flat and even. "So, An-To-Wee, in your old age you have taken up with dogs. Maybe both you and your warrior son, Blue Jay, are no longer brave men but squaws in paint only."

Blue Jay charged forward, knife dawn. An-To-Wee yelled, "*Stop*! You speak bravely white eyes. Let us see if you can remember our ways.

Allen breathed deeply. An-To-Wee had taken *his* bait. "So be it, great chief. Then it will be. Let us see who is the bravest. But according to our law, can I not cause the terms?" The village elders nodded in agreement.

An-To-Wee spoke. "You may choose. So say it."

Ho-Ta-Wa pointed to Jim Coogan. "It is he—first by the knife in the circle of death. How do you answer?" It was clear that Coogan did not like the choice.

"Let it be," said An-To-Wee. The village cheered and An-To-Wee held his hands up for silence. "But there is more. You will run the road of death."

Hugh struggled. "No Allen, No! They'll kill you, boy!" One of the braves choked off his words.

Ho-Ta-Wa spoke. "So be it. But on a condition. If I must endure this and win, then you must release the girl child and the old man."

"No!" shouted Blue Jay. "No! They must die!"

Ho-Ta-Wa laughed with scorn. "Ah! So you are afraid my bravery will win! Or is it, Blue Jay, that truth shall win?"

The look on Blue Jay's face told Allen that he understood.

"It is a shame," Allen continued, "for your people will not see the sport."

Immediately the entire village chanted, "Yes! Yes!

Yes!"

Then the Cheif spoke again. "It is our way, Blue Jay, but Ho-Ta-Wa will not be so lucky. If he should win, he may go free with the old man and the girl, but only for one sun. Then our braves will hunt them down." With that, An-To-Wee turned and struck his war spear to the sun. "Let the preparations begin!"

Danielle held on to Allen as he tried to quiet her. Hugh sat honing Allens knife. "Ain't no way, son. You can't get through the gauntlet. Ain't been but one man to live and speak of it—ole Dan'l Boone hisself. Let's take our chances. I'll start a fight and you grab one of them ponies."

Allen shook his head. "It's the only way, ole hoss. You stay close to this little gal. The whole village will be watchin'. If'n somethin' goes wrong—you run!"

The circle consisted of a fire pit about sixty feet round and the center had been cleaned of all sticks and rocks. Short spears had been driven into the ground, point up, within the circle. Anyone stumbling or falling would be instantly seared or critically impaled.

Ho-Ta-Wa was brought from the captive teepee after little Danielle had kissed his cheek and Hugh had winked nervously, to be stood naked before the ring of death. Across from him at the opposite side stood Jim Coogan. The entire village was screaming as squaws danced around the two, making gestures as to their manhood. Coogan was partially drunk and seemed to be enjoying the whole thing. While Ho-Ta-Wa stood facing is opponent, his eyes were the slate grey of anger.

An-To-Wee stepped to the fire ring with a torch as several braves splashed pitch over the firewood, now placed in the circular ditch. The torch lowered and flames leaped above Ho-Ta-Wa's head as he jumped to the center ring between two of the upright spears. His knife was poised in his left hand. Coogan then also jumped into the fire ring, screaming his definace. Each man circled between the spears, knowing that one must be dead before the flames died.

To Allen, facing his adversary, one giant thought exploded in his brain. Once again he shot back twenty years in time to the Cumberland stockade, lying in ashes, the body of his father hanging from the log gate. As the scene played out in his mind, rage grew to take its place—a rage that drew the slate grey eyes to narrow slits and caused each muscle to tense.

Allen's Indian training emerged and Ho-Ta-Wa took over the body of Allen Crosstree. The muscles relaxed, the eyes opened to view every spear head and take in even Coogan's slightest movements. His heart calmed to a comfortable rhythm, and his mind pinpointed on Coogan's knife. It seemed that Ho-Ta-Wa floated between the spear heads, making it difficult for Coogan to find a target. The spirit of Ho-Ta-Wa completely ignored its counterpart and total concentration evolved.

Coogan crouched in his rage as a spear tip penitrated the back of his thigh. He jumped forward screaming, and slashed at Ho-Ta-Wa. His momentum carried him into Ho-Ta-Wa's range and the warrior's knife sliced his shoulder as he miraculously fell between the upright spears. Ho-Ta-Wa jumped backwards, the flames searing his back. He winced as he smelled his own flesh.

Coogan was bleeding badly from both the shoulder wound and the spear, but his strength was unbelievable as he cautiously stalked his opponent, the skinner's knife gleaming in the firelight. Smoke from the pitch fire caused each man to cough and tears to stream down their faces.

They sparred and thrust and each time both suffered cuts and stabs by the razor sharp spears. Both were growing tired after a time, as the flames lowered enough that now they could see the tribe in a circle around the fire. There was no sound as An-To-Wee and his people waited for the final thrust that would declare a winner and a loser.

Hugh Applegate had comforted Danielle and now made ready his escape should Ho-Ta-Wa be the loser. He was slitting the skin hide at the back of the teepee when Danielle asked, "What are you doing, Mister Applegate?"

"We's gonna get outta here if'n somethin' goes amiss. You be ready to run if'n I give the sign."

"Ain't no use to do that, Mister Applegate," Danielle said with conviction. "Mister Crosstree's gonna get us outta here."

Hugh smiled hs toothless smile and suddenly found an unexplainable calmness about his entire body. "Dad burn it, child. I believe you is right." Immediately he abandoned his preparations and sat down beside her. They smiled at one another.

The thrust had come when Jim Coogan charged. Ho-Ta-Wa sidestepped and the skinning knife went home. As he jumped the fire ring in victory, the last flames were still flickering. He was exhausted, but for now he was the victor and the tribe would celebrate his victory even though he was a hated enemy.

That night, dancing and food was in abundance. Ho-Ta-Wa, Danielle and Hugh all sat in honor at An-

To-Wee's side. There was no mention of tomorrow, when Ho-Ta-Wa would run the gauntlet. For now, he was a hero and true to Indian custom, a celebration was in order. As Ho-Ta-Wa scanned the crowd, he noticed one face conspicuously missing. Blue Jay was nowhere to be seen.

An-To-Wee was every bit the host, demanding from the squaws that Ho-Ta-Wa be served the first choice bits of venison. As the pipe was passed, Danielle and Hugh were also honored. It was the Kickapoo custom. Even the braves who, only hours before had wanted his life, honored his presence. Ho-Ta-Wa played the game well, demanding quiet as he sang his victory chant and told tales of his bravery. The Indians hung on his every word.

As chief recipient of the honor of bravery, Ho-Ta-Wa excercised his right to ask questions of An-To-Wee. Else his spirit be lost to his lies, no Kickapoo would dare to lie to a brave warrior. An-To-Wee, therefore, answered with candor.

"Tell me, oh Great Chief, why do you seek my spirit?"

An-To-Wee grew grim as he answered. "Ho-Ta-Wa was chosen to be a brave and a Kickapoo warrior and he violated that trust."

"How so, oh Great Chief? Because I left your village?"

"No. For even our own braves leave to seek brave deeds. No, Ho-Ta-Wa, it is because you treacherously counted coup on Rapid Water and then you did not honor tribal law. You lay in wait for Blue Jay and with the white eyes old one there you tried to take his spirit."

Ho-Ta-Wa placed his hand on his breast while he spoke, the sign of total honesty. "You have been told wrongly, gallant chief. I broke tribal law by making a cooking fire with the old one here, even though I knew he was a white man. he told me of my white father and spoke the language long forgotten to my ears. Rapid Water entered the camp, hurling insults, but he was killed by the hatchet of my brother Blue Jay, who saw what was happening and gallantly saved my life when he saw Rapid Water attack. He had been watching at the forest's edge."

An-To-Wee stared in disbelief. "What you say is strange to my ears, Ho-Ta-Wa. Mark that you tell only truth."

"This is truth, my father. I am a warrior of honor!" Ho-Ta-Wa took a stern tone, and An-To-Wee, though perhaps he did not want to, felt respect.

"My brother Blue Jay was already in trouble with the tribal council because of his jealousy of Rapid Water, and he tried to persuade me to take the blame for Rapid Water's death. Though I was in part responsible, for breaking tribal law, I could not lie—not even for Blue Jay. We fought, and I thought I had killed him. He even sang his song of death. That was when I left the village for good. I could not return to you, having killed my own brother."

An-To-Wee stood, shouting to the crowd. "Bring me Blue Jay!"

A brave replied, "He is gone, Great Chief, to declare his bravery on the great war trail."

Ho-Ta-Wa's eyes bore deep into those of his adopted father. "Why, oh Great One, do you think Blue Jay took this time to leave the village?"

An-To-Wee's eyes clowded with deep sadness. "It saddens my heart even unto death to think that what you say about my son is true. But it matters not to your fate, for the decision has been made. Your life shall be

measured at the coming of the sun. I will deal with Blue
Jay in my own way." His words were almost a reverie and
Allen could feel the deep sadness coming from the great
man. He knew, also that the sadness was not for Blue Jay
alone but for his adopted son as well, that he mourned
the years of misunderstanding.

Ho-Ta-Wa embranced the great Kickapoo chief as
he spoke, a tribute in recognition of An-To-Wee's rule as
chief. Then he asked his next question.

"Why do you war against the whites? The great
general buys your furs and offers much at the coming of
the white rain."

"It was true before this time, brave Ho-Ta-Wa, but
no more. Not many suns ago, we were summond to Little
Turtle by a Delaware sent to us by the Miamis." An-To-
Wee clapped his hands, and an old squaw approached.
An-To-Wee spoke to her and she immediately left, to
return shortly with a packet. No emotion was shown on
the face of Ho-Ta-Wa, but he at once recognized it as
being the packet carried by the brave when he had
retrieved the war belt.

"This is what Little Turtle gave to me," An-To-Wee
said. He slowly opened the packet, displaying its contents. Inside were the scalp locks of two Kickapoo Indian
maidens. Alongside the scalps was a military button
from a 1st Dragoon tunic and a parchment marked with
the Miami sign.

"May I finger the Indian book, great Chief?" Ho-
Ta-Wa reached for the parchment as An-To-Wee
nodded consent. He bent towards the fire to read it.

"We have found the spirit shells of your squaws.
They have been counted by a white soldier. The Miamis
will avenge them by making war on the whites. The man

f the long knife will pay for his deed."

Allen studied the message for a long time, giving
imself precious moments to search his memory. It had
een during the hunting trip that Allen had first seen
Iugh Applegate. There had been ten braves along with
quaws to peel the hides and to keep the camp. Two of
hese had been Dark Fawn and her sister Little Squirrel.
'here had been an argument between Dark Fawn and
Blue Jay because he had learned that she had gone to
Rapid Water's teepee two summers before. Little
quirrel had intervened. She was known for her sharp
ongue. That was the last time he had seen the two, and
s he carefully examined the contents of the packet, he
ealized that he was looking at the scalp braids of Dark
Fawn and Little Squirrel. He felt deep sadness.

"It is Dark Fawn and her sister Little Squirrel, is it
aot?" Ho-Ta-Wa asked.

"Yes, and our hearts grieve for our maidens. The
white eyes have killed them and their deaths had to be
avenged! That is why we have fought. Our honor would
be tarnished if the Miamis avenged them for us."

Allen's next question was asked as his eyes searched
deep into An-To-Wee's. "Did you not plan for me to
come to the village? Was not the little white squaw taken
so that I would come, Father?"

An-To-Wee paused a long moment before answering, surveying the village and the mountains
beyond, silhouetted by the bright moonlight. Finally he
spoke.

"Yes, my white son. Only a few days before their
disappearance, Dark Fawn came to me. She told me she
and Little Squirrel had something they must tell me, and
that it began at the time of your leaving the village. She

said I must know for many were in danger." An-To-Wee
stopped, bowing his head. He was silent for so long that
Allen thought he might be dozing.

"Yes, father?" he said, breaking the silence.

An-To-Wee looked at Ho-Ta-Wa, then looked
away. "Blue Jay came to my tent at that moment and
Dark Fawn left quickly. She has not been a friend of
Blue Jay's ever since the time of Rapid Water, as you
may know. But soon after, she and Little Squirrel
disappeared and I had no way to find out what it was she
was going to tell me. It has troubled my heart. I admit I
wanted you at my fire, Ho-Ta-Wa, to tell me what you
know. My heart grieves that you may have already given
me part of the answer."

"I know not what she was going to tell you," Ho-Ta-
Wa answered, "but if I survive tomorrow I will do all in
my power to find out."

"Blue Jay," Allen thought to himself. "The answers
lie with Blue Jay." Blue Jay—whom Allen had seen in the
Miami village only days before. But Blue Jay was gone.

Ho-Ta-Wa turned towards the chief. "Great An-
To-Wee, my heart is heavy with the message of these
deaths. The answer is not clear to me, but is it possible
that you are wrong about what happend to them?"

An-To-Wee half-rose from his cross-legged seating
position.

"Do you doubt my word? Do not take advantage of
you honored place at my side!"

Allen touched his head to the ground in apology,
paying the form of the greatest humbleness. He knew
that at sunrise he had to run, and if he could find the
answer he knew that An-To-Wee would listen. As was
the custom, one who ran the row of death and survived
would forever be honored in the seven tribes. The

honored position would help him find the answers he sought.

Hugh and Ho-Ta-Wa had stayed awake most of the night, talking about all that had happened in the past five days and nights. Allen revealed to Hugh his suspicions about the packet shown to him by An-To-Wee, and Hugh searched his own memory back to the day he had met Allen. "Could it be that them two squaws seed what happened 'tween you and Blue Jay?" he asked.

"No way we can know, ole hoss, not until I get outta here and find Blue Jay and get me some answers."

"The more I ponder it, sonny, the more I worry about that there swamp and them tracks goin' in there. Reckon somethin' mighty strange is a goin' on down there."

"Jest hope that woman and boy is safe back there, Hugh. Reckon that's about the most important thing."

The dawn was fog-shrouded and caused a chill to the bone. Ho-Ta-Wa was prepared for his great run. Squaws tenderly oiled his body after his leggins were removed. Only a breech clout was worn. No one spoke, for it was forbidden.

As the faint streaks of light touched the teepee, beginning to burn off the fog, the ritual began. The oiling and greasing down was followed by a breakfast of partride eggs and blood raw venison. Allen ate with a hearty appetite while little Danielle Sullivan sat quietly watching. Allen noticed her look, and he gently rubbed her head.

"You be a good gal, now, and don't you fret none. Why, before the sun's dipped over yonder hill, we'll have you in your Mama's arms.

Danielle slowly stood. Then, in a burst of tears, she rushed into Allen's arms. Hugh gently pulled her back, It was a bad omen to touch one who faced trial.

Soon, a wild, eerie sound came across the village. The device used to make the sound was a stag horn finely scraped with rocks until it was paper-thin, then held between the palms. A brave would place his lips against his thumbs and blow. The sound was somewhat like the sound of a wounded eagle. It was the final tribute to the brave Ho-Ta-Wa, as well as the call to arms for the village braves.

Ho-Ta-Wa nodded to Hugh. Danielle had covered her face in fright as the two fearsome-looking bucks entered the teepee to escort Ho-Ta-Wa to the head of the row of death. This was not a prisoner escort, but one of honor. the two Indians had been selected by An-To-Wee as the two bravest of the tribe. As was decreed by law, they could not look upon Ho-Ta-Wa's face.

An-To-Wee was a model of splendor as he stood at the starting post, his head bonnet with its hawk feathers trailed for many yards behind him on the ground and his breast plate of porcupine quills reflected the sun's first rays like jewels of foxfire. His eyes were closed and his arms outstretched as he chanted the story of Ho-Ta-Wa, the bravest of braves. The entire village was motionless and not even the village dogs barked as drums gently transferred the story to the four winds over the creek and beyond.

Ho-Ta-Wa was a magnificent specimen standing before the great chief, his arms, legs and torso shining from the bear fat. His hair had been plaited on one side and the feather from the tail of the red hawk dangled over his left shoulder. A simple belt woven of horse hair entwined his right bicep. Each was a powerful totem. The feather indicated Ho-Ta-Wa's fleetness, for as a boy growing up in the village and later as a young brave, he was noted for his swiftness. It was said in An-To-Wee's legend, that as the red hawk, Ho-Ta-Wa would fly down the row of death. The legend continued, saying that, as the stallion, Ho-Ta-Wa's belt caused him to have great wind to run.

The drums stopped on their highest note and An-To-Wee walked to Ho-Ta-Wa's back. Ho-Ta-Wa was now facing the gauntlet. There before him in two rows was the most awesome sight Ho-Ta-Wa had even seen. Warriors stood in each line facing inward, approximately ten feet in between the two rows. Each brave wore his favored battle dress and full war paint. Yet no sound was heard. Allen's eyes glanced at the hands of the braves. Knives, war clubs and hatchets hung by thong handles waiting to be raised to strike the fatal blow upon Ho-Ta-Wa, who would run between the two rows. As Allen watched, his lips began to chant noiselessly. It was a strength chant, invoking the gods of bravery to make him fleet of foot.

Then his eyes widened at the sight. At the far end of the gauntlet, bound together, stood Danielle and Hugh, and Allen was suddenly proud. Both stood straight, looking towards Allen. Danielle was not crying. Allen knew the purpose of the two squaws standing behind them should he fail. The squaws would quickly, and without ceremony, club them to death. An-To-Wee again spoke.

"It has been done. The law of Em-O-Tee-Tee. Hear his chant as well as that of your braves who will cause his

spirit to fly." Then the tradition willed, An-To-Wee
lifted Ho-Ta-Wa's Hawk feather. Allen's muscles
tensed, knowing that as the feather fell against his neck
he was to run. Hatchets and clubs were raised and
Allen's toes dug into the hard-packed earth. He felt the
faintest whisper on his ear as the feather fell. Then Ho-
Ta-Wa ran.

It is still sopken, this legend of Ho-Ta-Wa, for even
today they say that Em-O-Tee-Tee grabbed up the brave
Ho-Ta-Wa and blew him as the giant wind down the row
of death onto the waiting arms of his friends.

Chapter 9

Mongo lay to the west and for Allen, Hugh and Danielle, who had to be carried, it was a hot and nerve-racking trek. In the distance, the crescendo of village drums could be heard declaring the feat of Ho-Ta-Wa and the Council law that he was to "go through without being harmed until the great ball of fire should rise again." Allen and Hugh both knew that at that very moment, braves hung back over the rim or beyond the trees waiting for the drum's signal that would declare the brave Ho-Ta-Wa and his companions open for the hunt. Great effort would be made to track them down, for the brave who's hatchet fell the great one would be assured of immortality.

When Allen and Hugh arrived carrying Danielle, they found the boy Aaron sitting by his Mother. He had been applying watercress poltices to her shoulder and the wet bucksin patches testified that he had drunk no water, but had used it for his Mother. He and his sister hugged one another and cried.

Mary Lou was feverish and at times talked out of her head. She only faintly recognized her daughter.

Danielle was frightened. "What's wrong with my Mama, Mister Ho-Ta-Wa? Is she gonna die?"

Allen scooped her up into his arms and answered gently. "We ain't gonna let her die, little 'un. She's gonna be jest fine."

Allen knew what must be done. Mary Lou needed

the white man's doctor and Cincytown was where the surgeon general's army hospital was. Yet he also knew that the war between Indians and whites must be stopped. Little Turtle had lied and Allen knew that Spanish forces now waited to move north as the tribes wrought murder upon the white settlers. He was certain the answer lay in the Mongo Swamp and he expressed his thought to Hugh.

Evening had fallen and still they discussed their plight. Allen had finished the sassafras poltice for Mary Lou's shoulder and she now lay sleeping. Aaron and Danielle lay huddled together watching their mother and wincing at each low moan of pain. When Allen had finally made up his mind, he spoke.

"Hugh, ole hoss, where is the likely place fer them braves to hunt us down come t'marrow sunup?"

The old scout rubbed his chin. "Why I reckon the onliest place they *won't* trod is into that swamp."

Aaron had raised up as he heard Hugh's comment. "Beggin' your pardon, Ho-Ta-Wa, that ain't rightly so. Late yestiddy I seen an Injun goin' into that there swamp."

Allen became alert at Aaron's words. "Air you certain, boy? Tell me. What did this here buck look like?"

"Cain't be sure about that, Sir," the boy replied. "Hit was comin' on dark, but I seed his leggins with the hawk feathers in 'em."

"Blue Jay!" exalimed Allen. "Member, Hugh? He was a 'wearing' them leggings when me and Coogan fought!"

"Yep. The same," Hugh replied, crawling over to Aaron. "Remember now, for all you's worth. Where 'bouts did he go in at?"

Aaron pointed into the darkness. "Over there, Mister Hugh, betwixt the outline of them two big sycamores. Hugh glanced at Allen, though in the darkness he couldn't see his face. "Reckon, Ho-Ta-Wa, ole Blue Jay skedaddled befor'n the truth showed up at the village. Peers he's more afeared of his Daddy than ole Ha-In-Mott."

"Or maybe he's not alone in there, ole Hoss," Allen responded.

They were silent for awhile, listening to the night sounds coming from the swamp. Allen stood, coming closer to Hugh and Aaron. "Hugh, if we could cross this here swamp, where would we come out?"

Hugh thought for a long moment before answring.

"Well now. I 'spect we'd come out 'bout the Tanglewood Pond."

Allen knew that place as being south. It was an area with short hickory stubs growing entwined. Some called it "Shelter Grove" and it was in a direct line south to Vincins and east in direct line to Greenville's post. From there on, it was but a day into the new stockade at Cincytown.

"Well now, ole hoss, I reckon hows if'n we was to cross over this here mud hole that you could get the lady and her younguns on down to Cincytown lot quicker. They ain't not Kicks or Miamis gonna go in that swamp yonder and it would take 'em two, three days a'scouting' to pick up your tracks. By then you could be coolin yer heels in that there stream at Cincytown, huh?"

"Lord A'mighty, Ho-Ta-Wa. You's plain teched. Why, I ain't never been across that there mud pond. Anyways, how we gonna get this here woman across? She ain't fittin' to walk. I heered tales that they's moccasin rattlers bigger'n a man's leg in thar."

Allen studied the darkness, then spoke. "Heck, hoss, she ain't gonna walk. We's gonna push her and the younguns through that old mud hole with a water toboggan."

"Water toboggan? What you talkin' about, Allen Crosstree? How's we gonna do a thing like that?"

Allen began his explanation, and Hugh began to nod. "Might work, Sonny", he said finally. "It jest might work."

The two scouts began to work. First they chose two long, straight birches, carefully making a platform of willow and grapevines. No word was spoken as the construction continued far into the night. It was difficult to see, but the two were determined and a little desperate.

By first light, the shallow raft was deep into the swamp, with Mary Lou and her children on the platform. Allen and Hugh shoved and pushed the craft across water, mud and swamp reed grass. Both men were near the end of their stamina and strength, but they knew the urgency of reaching the other side. Aaron and Danielle stayed awake and each time a wildcat screamed or a reed rustled they clasped one another, but neither screamed out.

As light streaked the morning sky, drums in the distance started their message of death as braves ran headlong down forest paths seeking Ho-Ta-Wa and his people, only to stop at the swamp's edge in legendary fear.

A travis was hastily constructed with rawhide straps that slung around Hugh's middle, and Mary Lou was gently placed on it in a bed of pine boughs by Allen. His gentleness moved the frontiersman until a tear slid down his mud-crusted cheek. Allen stepped back.

"All right, ole hoss, she's all your'n. Go south and east."

"Don't worry about me, none," Hugh answered. "I know trails through this country no white man's ever been on."

Allen nodded, then turned to Aaron and Danielle. He knelt, hugging both youngsters. "Now you younguns mind Hugh. Your Mama's gonna be all right, but you'll have to move swift and quiet. Don't do nothin' to slow him down. You hear?"

"We will, Ho-Ta-Wa, I promise we will. Here, Mister Applegate, let me help pull." Aaron's small frame ducked under the madeshift harness while Danielle stood beside the travis, a wet rag held to her mother's forehead.

"Please, Mister Crosstree. Come with us. I'm scared." The little girl's voice trembled.

"Aw, shucks, honey. You ain't really gonna be scared. Why, ole Hugh here'll have you in Cincytwon in a wink." Allen hugged her, the grey eyes knowing and tender.

Mary Lou moaned then and opened her eyes. Allen knelt at her side. "How you feelin'?" he asked gently.

Mary Lou didn't answer, but simply reached up her arms. Allen embraced her, and Aaron thought he saw tears in Allen's eyes. Mary Lou had already lapsed again into unconsciousness when they were ready to leave.

"See you in Cincytown, ole Hoss," Allen said, raising his hand in the Indian peace sign.

Hugh replied. "Weuns will be there. Go keerful, Ho-Ta-Wa."

As Allen turned away, he could hear the scraping of the travis as Hugh began his long pull. His heart was heavy with worry aobut them, and he almost decided to

turn around and go with them, but he steeled himself.
Hugh could handle it, and he had something to do that
couldn't wait.

Recrossing the swamp was done swiftly and midway
he started patiently criss-crossing, working his way
towards the middle of what he thought might be the hub.
He was surprised when in a few minutes he began to
strike solid ground with his moccasins.

"Well, I'll be blamed!" he whispered to himself.
This ain't no swamp here." As far as he could see ahead,
there was solid ground. In the distance, drums carried
the message. "Ho-Ta-Wa and his people have been
swollowed up by the swamp. The spirit of Ha-In-Mott
has them."

Allen breathed deep. It had now been hours since
he had left Hugh. By now, the would be a long way down
the trail. Suddenly, Ho-Ta-Wa seemed to become totally
immobile. Smoke! He smelled the faint acid odor of
burning sycamore. No ghost need a fire!

As silent as a breeze, Ho-Ta-Wa left his Allen
Crosstree self behind again and drifted through the
tangle of scrub and fallen sycamores until he was clsoe
enough for the smoke to become the faintest flicker of a
dry cook fire. He could see figures moving about. Some
appeared to be in uniform, but they were not uniforms
that Ho-Ta-Wa had seen before. He knew he would need
to get nearer. Turning his eyes up towards the sun, he
reckoned the time to be near late evening. In another
hour, he would feel darkness begin to descend and the
horned owl would start his flight. Then he could move
closer. Until then, Ho-Ta-Wa lay perfectly still while
large black mosquitos feasted on his neck where traces of
the bear grease lingered.

Ho-Ta-Wa had dozed and a shout from the swamp

made him tense to full awakening. He slowly slid his arms beneath him at the center of his body in order to raise up slowly to see better.

The high-pitched rattle froze him halfway in his effort to raise himself. Before him , approximately two feet away from his eyes, lay coiled the deadly Mo-Ta-To-Tee, the swamp rattler. The snake was thick and nearly four feet long, the head as large as both Ho-Ta-Wa's fists. It was raised in the position of death and as Ho-Ta-Wa looked into Mo-Ta-To-Tee's milky eyes, he knew that the slightest muscle movement would bring the razor- sharp fangs forward in a blurr to sink deep into his face or throat.

Ho-Ta-Wa had at times, while living in the village, experience immobility for long periods of time, never as much as closing the eyelids. It was part of the training required before a man-child could claim his place as a warrior. Those years of training took over his every thought. He could emit no fear, for he knew that the forked tongue sought heat and the pale milky eyes sought movement. He knew, too, that he could not even sweat, so he conjured up in his min'd eye great drifts of white rain. The image was so intense that he could feel the chill moving up his body. The forearm and bicep muscles cramped into strong knots of rope, while the steel grey eyes never left the head of Mo-Ta-To-Tee. The rattlers whirred as the black tongue sought out its prey.

Ho-Ta-Wa knew that darkness and its chill would drive the snake to his lair, but darkness was still far away. His muscles knotted even tighter. He used the utmost of his Indian discipline to keep his thoughts steady. He knew that should be abandon his Indian self, the spiritual change would instantly cuase Mo-Ta-To-Tee to strike.

A faint blur in the corner of his eye flashed meaning to his brain, and his hopes of escape rose. The soft grey-brown creature reared to its back legs, its large liquid eyes glued to the rattler. There was no curiosity, only intent in the small animal's eyes as the sensitive whiskers around the pointed nose twitched. Ho-Ta-Wa's inner self smiled as the furry death stalker sat patiently waiting for his moment to strike. Of all the animals of the forest, only two dared callenge Mo-A-To-Tee to the death. One was the eagle, the spirit bird who's talons could rip an Injun pony open at the first swoop. The other was no more than a rat-sized blur of motion, but all feared his lightening speed that ended in the spine or juglar vein being caught like a vice in the small fangs, bringing death. Man himself feared him, giving him wide range. But at this moment, to Ho-Ta-Wa, the wolverine had come from the spirits.

His charge came so swiftyly that Ho-Ta-Wa actually did not see it. One moment, the rattlers sounded their rhythm and the next, the furry ball had Mo-A-To-Tee directly back of the head as struggle between the two made small thudding sounds on the ground. Ho-Ta-Wa gently lowered his torso to the ground, trembling. The wolverine shook the snake until the head came off, then, ignoring the man totally, he feasted on the wriggling remains. When done, he casually rambled off as if the incident had never happened.

The camp was fairly large, with a long structure thrown up as a breast works facing the north of the swamp. Soldiers, now identified as Spaniards, sat around the fire eating from a large pot hanging over rock coals. The aroma reminded Ho-Ta-Wa that he had not eaten since the last sun.

Carefully, he eased himself towards the breastworks, seeing that no guards were about. It was evident that the superstitions made the camp safe. The breastworks was about the height of a tall brave and the bottom log lay half-submerged in the swamp grass and mud. Above it where the next log lay upon it, a broken limb separated the two logs, leaving a crack. By lying on his side, facing the logs, Ho-Ta-Wa had a perfect view of the entire camp. To the right of the fire was a lean-to and as the fire flared with each new log thrown on, he could see various army equipment stacked about. Guns with wide ends were stacked there as was powder and shot—enough to Allen's thinking to arm several thousand soldiers. Yet there were no more than twenty thirty people in the camp.

To the right of the lean-to, a small three-walled cabin stood, the front draped with a large canvas. A bear grease light flickered inside, giving off weird dancing shadows across the large sycamores standing about. Ho-Ta-Wa watched the cabin intently. Whoever had come in no doubt was in the cabin. He was surprised at the quietness of the camp. The men were well-disciplined.

The canvas parted and as Ho-Ta-Wa watched, out stepped Blue Jay and one of Jim Coogan's men. Behind them came Little Turtle and a tall, dark-bearded man in uniform. It was apparent he was a man of rank, for the soldiers all rose as if one and saluted. The group each filled a plate of food and retired once again to the cabin. Ho-Ta-Wa thought of the message he had taken from the Delaware who had put the arrow in Mary Lou's shoulder. This could be the officer who signed the message. The Spanish were much closer than anyone imagined! But General Wilkerson was not here, though the message made it clear that he was involved. The thought crossed Allen's mind that the General, being the same kind of coward as Lieutenant Price, may well have fled the scene entirely.

There was absolutely no doubt now that Blue Jay was involved. The anger in Ho-Ta-Wa rose. The Kickapoo had been sold out by An-To-Wee's own blood son, and there had to have been some kind of trick to have brought An-To-Wee into alliance with Little Turtle.

Ho-Ta-Wa decided that the cabin held the secrets he sought, so he carefully worked his way towards the back of the cabin. The chinking was made of saw grass and mud. After close examination, Allen found a loose piece of chinking and very carefully he removed a small section from between the cottonwood logs so as to see inside.

Sitting at a large, elaborate table, which looked to be made of ironwood, sat Chief Little Turtle. The Spaniard and Blue Jay were standing. Back of Blue Jay was one of Coogan's men. The entire group was talking in sign except occasional interruptions when the officer would talk to Coogan's man in a strange lingo.

Little Turtle sat quietly until the two men had finished talking. Then by sign, he spoke to Blue Jay. "Why has not An-To-Wee led his village to war?"

Blue Jay responded. "He is grieved that the black beards do not come to his village to pow-wow. He suspects something goes between the Miamis and the black beards."

Little Turtle rose. "It is you who made our pact. Yet only a handful of your warrior s make war. It is because of you that our war belt is now gone."

Blue Jay moved up, his right hand closing on the handle of his hatchet.

"Ho-Ta-Wa is the one who counted coup on the

Delaware. I have kept my bargain for your promise—that I will stand second only to you, Little Turtle, as leader among the seven tribes. It was I, Blue Jay, who supplied the braids of our squaws so you might rouse An-To-Wee to war."

Little Turtle's smile was equal to an Indian sneer. "But do not forget, Blue Jay, that I know why you killed the squaws. They had overheard all we had said that day. They knew of our plans with the black beards and they knew of your dark secret about Ho-Ta-Wa. You were trying to save your own skin—Blue Jay! You were fortunate to make all of it work for your own totem. Now your white eyes brother has escaped from your squaw braves. It is he also who has the black beard message to the white eyes General. Ho-Ta-Wa was in your village. Why did you not kill him?"

Blue Jay was enraged as he answered. "Had you not killed the white-haired Price and his Sergeant, we could have traded!"

The officer stood, and in sign he spoke. "Come now. We are all brothers. We are not of the white eyes. Our chief offers much gold and horses but the white eyes must be removed as promised. This Ho-Ta-Wa is not important. With all the tribe looking for him he will never make it to Cincytown. It matters not about the message. What is important, Blue Jay, is for you to convince your chief to war against Chi-Ka-Go. Our army waits now to come into your lands."

Little Turtle showed anger as he spoke. "We, the Miami, have done as promised. If An-To-Wee will not war, we will burn his village. The whiskey man is dead and my braves crave the white fire. We must do something to anger An-To-Wee into battle against the whites. My scouts say that the General Wayne, has been shut away because of the things General Wilkerson told the King Chief far away. If we act quickly, we will have time to take all the forts before the white army can again be ready to fight.''

Ho-Ta-Wa felt rage. The Kickapoo were being used as pawns by the power-seeking Little Turtle and by these Spaniards. He must get to An-To-Wee. The Sauk, Delaware, Illinois and others would fight if An-To-Wee did. Somehow the treachery had to be revealed.

As Ho-Ta-Wa listened and watched, the argument grew intense between Little Turtle and Blue Jay. Again the officer spoke to Coogan's man in the strange lingo, and the man nodded his understanding. He continued talking to the Indians in sign.

"We must take action. Then it is agreed we will force An-To-Wee to take the war path at least against Fort Dearborn, for it is the Kickapoo winter grounds.''

"The deaths of the two squaws was blamed on the white eyes,'' Little Turtle said. "It would take a deed equal to that to anger An-To-Wee and force him to do as we want.''

Blue Jay abandoned the sign and shouted. "Stop this! It is not the way and I will not again violate my tribe's law. Not for a thousand horses and Little Turtle's honored position itself!''

The officer looked at Little Turtle, then at Coogan's man. "It was not you, Blue Jay, that we ask to do this thing.''

Blue Jay half-rose, suspicion in his eyes. His hand again tightened upon his hatchet. Coogan's man had stepped closer and Ho-Ta-Wa's lips moved in soundless chant for Blue Jay's death song. Blue Jay never had the opportunity, for the hatchet was buried deep into his skull.

Quickly, the officer went to a chest standing beside the wall. He gave Coogan's man a pair of army boots, Continental army boots, and several other articles. Some were blood-stained. He spoke in the strange language as he instructed the man. Then he turned to Little Turtle.

"At first day," he said, "we will have this one take Blue Jay's body to the Chief of the Kickapoo. With these things, he can swear that Blue Jay was attacked and killed by Wayne's soldiers who were in hiding. He will tell An-To-Wee that we will help his braves with guns and powder and with whiskey also. We will say that the white eyes soldiers escaped to Fort Dearborn at Chi-Ka-Go. Then the Kickapoo will attack while your braves go north to the great lake at Detroit." The officer poured three large pewter cups of whiskey and they all drank.

Ho-Ta-Wa lay still. His heart was heavy for Blue Jay. He had become a victim of his hate, his lies and his greed. He watched as the wrapped Blue Jay in a Miami blanket while Coogan's man prepared to take Blue Jay to his village. Allen knew then what he would do. Quietly, he slid away from the back wall into the swamp, making his way towards the swamp's edge. He knew that he would have to intercept the man near the swamp, for still An-To-Wee's braves hunted the elusive Ho-Ta-Wa. He had followed a trail of sorts from the camp to the swamp's edge and it was there he made his place for the night. He was reasonably certain Coogan's man would follow that same trail. His body was aching from fatigue, and rest would revive his spirit.

As he lay down on the bed of moss, his mind went to Mary Lou. She was a fine woman, he thought, but he wondered if she could survive the frontier. Her recent experience had no doubt left her with the desire to return to her people on the banks of the sea. This made him sad, for he knew now that he loved her and the children.

As he continued his watch, he could hear the drums in the distance. The hunt for Ho-Ta-Wa still continued. It would be difficult to reach An-To-Wee, but he knew there was no choice. But lying back in the moss, the concentration drained away and he slowly relaxed into sleep.

As Allen awoke, faint streaks of dawn could be seen through the willows to the east and fog rose in lazy clouds. It was an omen of good things to come. He again heard the rustle of steps which had awakened him, and he concentrated to determine the direction from where they came. Allen moved closer to the narrow swamp trail. He had chosen his hiding place carefully behind a large sycamore where he could see the entire area without being easily detected.

He crouched as the Coogan man came into view, pulling the blanket-shrouded body of Blue Jay on top of two peeled cottonwood logs tied together with vines. By the body lay several pewter jugs. They would contain the raw liquid that cause brave warriors to become as screaming squaws. It would soon be time to move over the great creek and beyond. The white man had already poisoned the land. But first things first.

The man was of medium build but muscular. His muscles corded beneath buckskins as he pulled the log float onto dry ground. The man scanned the area briefly, so briefly in fact that it was obvious he felt no need to be careful. This was sacred legend ground. He pulled the float up again. Then, as an afterthought, he kicked the wrapped bundle, cursing as he did so. Ho-Ta-Wa's knife came out, but then he gently slid it back into the pony skin scabbard. "Not yet," he thought, "not yet."

Coogan's man passed very near to Allen as he turned on to a faint trail leading towards the west. There was a perplexed look on Allen's face as he watched. Soon the man was back, leading a black and white spotted Indian pony. That answered Allen's question as he once again became Ho-Ta-Wa. He would have to be total Indian now.

The buckskin-clad man loaded the corpse of Blue Jay across the back of the pony, first putting the blanket over the horse's back. The horse shied at his burden, for the smell of death was there.

It was then that Ho-Ta-Wa stepped from behind the sycamore onto the path, knife drawn. At first the man did not see him, having turned back to guide the pony over a fallen birch log. When he turned back, there stood the savage Ho-Ta-Wa, fearsome and tall, a hawk's feather dangling over his left shoulder. The pony shied as his leader came to a sudden stop. There was fear in the man's eyes as he recognized the legendary man before him, but he recovered his composure quickly and gave the palm-out sign of peace. Ho-Ta-Wa did not reply, but stood staring into the man's eyes. The leader of the horse then spoke in sign.

"Is it you, Ho-Ta-Wa, the Spirit of the Wind? I am glad you found us." Still Allen did not respond and the man continued. "I am lost and seek the village of An-To-Wee of your village tribe."

The grey eyes of Ho-Ta-Wa drilled into the speaker, who stuttered as he continued, talking and signing at the same time. "I . . . I . . . I," then he signed. "I have found the son of An-To-Wee during the moon. White soldiers have slain him. I am trying to return his spirit to his people."

Allen answered by sign. "Yes, I am Ho-Ta-Wa of the Kickapoo. Where was Blue Jay found?"

The man replied, "near the white man's road."

"Ah, so you crossed the swamp then. Did you see the spirit of Ha-In-Mott?"

The Coogan man hesitated, then spoke. "No. I did not, but I heard strange noises. I am glad I am out of there." Slowly, his hand eased to his hatchet. He knew that this legendary man did not believe him.

Then Ho-Ta-Wa spoke as Allen, in his own language. "You are a liar. I watched you tomahawk Blue Jay. You and Little Turtle and the black beard officer."

The frontiersman charged, his hatchet drawn and screaming, "You lousy, half-breed son of . . . ."

Ho-Ta-Wa's knife slashed across the buckskin shirt and a faint red line appeared as the man went down. Instantly, Ho-Ta-Wa was on him, his hair gripped tightly in his left hand, pulling the head backwards until the thick neck bulged. He spoke as he yanked the head back in a grip of steel.

"You got one chance, Pilgrim, and only one, or I'll lift your hair as you watch. We're goin' to An-To-Wee now—me and you and Blue Jay."

The man stiffened and tried to wriggle free, but the grip tightened and the knife edge lay at the hair line of the forehead. Ho-Ta-Wa continued. "Your changes with An-To-Wee are better than with me if'n I decide to move this here knife and if'n the Chief don't kill you I will unless you speak up." Slowly, he released his grip and the man fell forward on the trail, grasping for breath. Finally he spoke. "I ain't to blame for this. Little Turtle said he'd kill me in the pit if'n I didn't do it, and you know An-To-Wee ain't gonna let me go!"

"Get up, you scum." Ho-Ta-Wa lifted the man by his hair. Quickly he tied the man to the pony's tail by braiding the hair around his wrist.

"For god's sake, you're white! You cain't do this! I'm a bleedin' bad!" The man was crying but Ho-Ta-Wa ignored him, walking to the front of the pony and, taking up the rawhide lariat, he angrily jerked the halter and the pony jumped forward, pulling Coogan's man off his feet. As the man screamed, Ho-Ta-Wa deliberately stepped out faster. At that moment he could never remember hate for the white man equal to that he felt now. Yes, when this was over, he would cross over the great Creek and go beyond and if Mary Lou wanted to go back to the shores of the sea then he would have to go alone.

The drums beat widly as Ho-Ta-Wa, leading the pony with its burden and the ponly leading the Coogan man was intercepted by a band of several Kickapoo brave. The warriors blocked the trail as Ho-Ta-Wa approached. They were mumbling and raising their hatchets in mock kill. Ho-Ta-Wa never faltered but led the pony through the band. The braves then saw the body of Blue Jay, now rigid in death. They were startled and drew back, chanting the death song. Then they saw the white man tied to the pony's tail and their screams filled the air as they dodged in and out, pretending to strike the man with their hatchets. He was terrified an as he stumbled, he desperately tried to keep on his feet. To pull too hard on the tail meant death by the hooves of the pony. In all of this Ho-Ta-Wa never looked to right or left nor did he falter in his march—not until he reached the village limits, standing where he had stood only three days before, awaiting his fight in the ring of fire and his run through the row of death.

Ho-Ta-Wa reverently pulled the dead Blue Jay from the pony's back. Then, as tradition dictated, he drew his knife, muzzled the pony's head with his hand and cut the juglar vein of the animal, with the man still tied to its tail. Then he chanted the story of Blue Jay's treachery and the story of his death while An-To-Wee looked on in sad understanding. The entire village had silently ringed the gruesome scene with An-To-Wee standing at their head, seeing and hearing all that was said. When Ho-Ta-Wa had finished, the pony thrashed his last breath away. The man tied to his tail was unconscious from the flying hooves, and he was gently picked up by several squaws. He would not be allowed to die—not this way.

An-To-Wee strode forward in all his mangificence. Ho-Ta-Wa could see his grief. Then he spoke. "Brave Ho-Ta-Wa, you have brought me much sadness. It is I who must now sing of Blue Jay's wrong. But you have also given me joy in your bravery. Come, let us smoke the pipe and eat of the spirits."

Ho-Ta-Wa then left the body standing before An-To-Wee and Allen Crosstree took its place as he spoke. "I take nothing from this village and I go as a white eyes. Part of me will always be as Ho-Ta-Wa, and I will cherish always your gifts as a father. What Blue Jay has done is done. It is my people and Little Turtle who must sing in shame, but I am of the white eyes and I must stand as their brave also. I leave to you the one who took Blue Jay's spirit in his weakness. It is for you to decide."

An-To-Wee placed his left hand on Allen's left shoulder, his fingers touching the hawk feather. His voice was strong as he spoke.

"We will bury Blue Jay in the Land of the Spirits. Then we will return to the banks of the great lake. You say you are of the white eyes. This will never be, for your bravery came as Ho-Ta-Wa and the drums shall tell it as so. Our lives are entwined by blood and our moccasins will one day again walk upon the same trail. Go in peace, Ho-Ta-Wa."

Softly, the entire village began to chant the parting song as Ho-Ta-Wa turned his back and faced the south and Cincytown.

Chapter 10

Cincinnati, as Cincytown had come to be called by some, was full of soldiers. Some still wore the bandanges proclaiming their battle with the Indians at Fort Miami. The mud and log village rambled from the hills down to the water's edge where spring rains now caused the river to look like a long brown snake. Cooking fires had been built, seemingly at random, with the smoke lying in thick layers between the hills. As Allen Crosstree made his way along the river's mud bank and then up the main street, his nostrils flared at the odor of unwashed humans, body waste and burned venison stew. He felt closed in and as if he were suffocating. The grey eyes closed to narrow slits as he passed the whiskey tents where soldiers, hunters and other assorted riff-raff stood in line to drink to rot gut whiskey. Once again, he was reminded of the day he had killed the Frenchman and of Mary Lou and Zeb Sullivan.

On the hill above the river, the Continentl flag flew and beneath it the standard of the Continental Army. Allen made his way between pack strings and the human flow of bodies towards the stockade.

He mounted the log stairs only to be stopped at the top by a solider with his rifle thrust forward.

"Halt!" he demanded.

Allen eyed the soldier and could see uncertainty in the young man's eyes. "State your business and who you wish to see," the young man said.

Allen rubbed his chin before speaking. "Well, soldier boy, I don't rightly know. I got a message for General Wayne. Is he here?"

"Yes, Sir," the boy replied. "He's under house arrest and the hearin' is in progress. What might your name be, Sir?"

Allen smiled. "Need to let the General know Ho-Ta-Wa's here."

The grip tightened on the rifle. "Sorry. No Injuns allowed."

Before the boy could take further action, a loud war whoop sounded behind him, coming from the doorway. The rifle dropped to the steps, accidentally firing, and Allen scrambled to the mud.

"Ho-Ta-Wa! You old crow bait!" There on the top step stood Hugh Applegate, laughing. "You be a sight for sore eyes, boy. You and that soldier boy a'wollowin' in that there mud."

Allen stood, brushing mud from his bucksins. "Hugh Applegate you done sceered me half outta a years growth!" Allen bounded up the steps and hugged the old frontiersman, while the young soldier kept pleading, "Wait! Wait! You ain't allowed in there!"

Colonel Armstrong rebuked the young soldier and winked at Allen and Hugh. "Crosstree, this crazy old coot kept sayin' you'd be here. We didn't believe him. Come. Come on in. We've a lot to talk about. I expect General Wayne's gonna be might pleased that you've come."

Allen stood still, eyeing Hugh. "Where's Mary Lou and the younguns?" he asked.

Hugh laughed. "Why, they's fine. Tell you all about it in a shake. Come on. The General's inside. That snake Wilkerson . . ."

Allen seemed surprised. "What's this about General Wayne?" he asked. "Didn't you give the packet to the General?"

"Heck no, Sonny. I was savin' that till you got there. Come on."

Allen grabbed Hugh's arm. "Now jest one blame minute, Hugh Applegate. How'd you know I was gonna be comin' at all?"

Hugh grinned his toothless grin. "The drums, boy, the drums. Ain't you ever heered of the Injun telegraph? I've been a'slippin' outta this here crowd purty regular up in them hills yonder where I could hear. Word got here afore you did, boy."

General Wilkerson sat in the large office of the Secretary of the Army. The Secretary was a large man with a hugh red beard and it was obvius that he was angry. Hugh and Allen entered unnoticed while the Secretary was speaking. "You say, General Wilkerson, that General Wayne was derelict in his duties as commander at Fort Miami?"

General Wilkerson nodded. "Yes, Sir. I forewarned the General of impending trouble with the Miamis and he refused to hear me out. My aide, Lieutenant Price, who died in battle, God rest his soul, had scouted out the enemy. I advised General Wayne to abandon the fort. We all knew it was useless as a frontier post."

"You realize," the Secretary said, "that your report does not conform to other officers under General Wayne's command."

"That is a simple matter to explain, Sir," Wilkerson replied, as calm and unruffled as if nothing were amiss. "They were advising the General. They are as much at fault as he is, and they are backing up his story."

Allen and Hugh were still unnoticed as General Wilkerson continued his charges against General Wayne. The Secretary conferred with several officers also sitting at the table. It was clear that the men were impressed with Wilkerson's confidence in his story.

Colonel Armstrong's signal attracted the Secretary's attention from across the room as he glanced up. At the Secretary's beckoning, the Colonel approached the table, whispering to the Secretary and the officers.

General Wilkerson moved in his seat, apparently irritated at the courtesy being shown to one of Wayne's loyal officers. After a few moments of whispered consultation, the Secretary rose and banged the table with his gavel. Wilkerson jumped slightly in his chair, startled by the sound.

"This hearing will take a thirty-minute recess. General Wilkerson, you will please remain seated." The secretary signaled to Allen and Hugh. "Gentlemen, please step forward."

Wilkerson whirled, his face suddenly ashen as he recognized the pair.

"Crosstree!" he said. "Where did you come from?"

Allen eyed the General with obvious contempt.

"Why'd ya ask, General. Didn't ya spect to ever see me again?"

"Why .... why .... I heard that you had fallen to them savages ... I'm mightly glad you're safe. Now you can tell them .... Mister Secretary, this scout can tell ...."

"Save your palaverin', Wilkerson. We intend a'speaking' to that fellar there." It was Hugh speaking and there was acid in his voice.

Allen and Hugh met the review board in another part of the building and each frontiersman recalled all that he had seen, heard and done over the past two weeks. Then Allen threw the Spanish packet on the table in front of the Secretary and Hugh gave him the Miami war belt.

"There's your proof, Mister. That there snake out there that you call 'General' ain't fittin' to be here on the frontier, and you best be don' somethin' about it afore'n somebody slits his gizzard and afore he causes more trouble." There was anger in Allen's tone as he spoke.

"We will, Mister Crosstree, we will. I promise you. But let's let the General hang himself." The Secretary stood as he picked up the contents of the packet and the war belt.

"Mister Crosstree . . . Mister Applegate . . . . we are forever in your debt. The frontier needs men like you."

The Secretary than turned to Colonel Armstrong, who had been present during the meeting. "Colonel, go fetch General Wayne please." The Colonel winked at Allen and Hugh and smiled.

As the Colonel spoke, he saluted smartly. "Yes Sir, Mister Secretary. Yes *Sir*!"

The hearing lasted a few brief moments longer. Panic had overcome General Wilkerson as he faced General Wayne and the Spanish document was read aloud. His face grew ashen again as Allen told of Lieutenant Price and Sergeant Loomis and their death at the Miami village. Wilkerson was led away under guard at the conclusion of the hearing.

General Wayne approached Allen and Hugh, a broad smile on his face. "Crosstree, thank you. Thank you very much. And you, Mister Applegate."

"Glad to oblige, General. Now best I be goin'. Important business to attend to," said Allen.

"Yes. Even under arrest I heard the gossip. She's at the Surgeon's building. Mind if I join you? I'm walkin' that way myself."

Allen nodded. Hugh excused himself, looking a little embarrassed.

"Crosstree," the General began, as they walked across the grounds, "come back to the Fort with me as my chief scout. Bring the lady and her children along. We'll pay you well and we'll build a bigger and better Fort this time on the banks of the Saint Joe. You can live in peace now that the army's on its way to Mongo Swamp and Wilkerson's gonna be behind bars. We can live peacefully. My agent will be on his way today to An-To-Wee and the scouting report says the Little Turtle has retreated north towards the lakes.

Allen smiled as he answwered. "Sorry, General. I reckon that someday Fort Miami will be as big maybe as Cincytown but it ain't for me. I've spent my life in the woods and livin' in a fort jest don't somehow seem natural."

The General interrupted. "But what about that woman and those children. Surely they can't be expected to roam the woods."

"You right, General, and I don't know right off if'n she'll go with me. But this here's a big country and more and more folks will be comin'. Peers I'd be more useful if'n I broke ground over the big creek and beyond so's others could take up land. Why, ole Hugh told me that beyond the big creek was mountains a man couldn't see the tops of and I am to see'em. Then someday, I'll find jest the place. No whiskey tents, no generals, jest God's place, where my woman and I can raise our younguns.

That is, if'n she'll have the likes of me.''

"Well, I wish you good luck with that, Crosstree. Wish you'd reconsider and come with me, though.''

A troubled look passed over Allen's face. "What about Hugh, General? He's gettin' mighty old.''

"Don't you worry none about that old bait. He's goin' as my hunter. I'll watch after him. Have you told him yet?''

"Yep," Allen answered.

They were at the Surgeon's building, and the two men parted with a smile and a wave.

The Surgeon General's hospital was little more than some logs thrown up with rows of board beds on each side. Corn shuck mattresses lay piled in one corner, the brown stains on them testifiying of the pain, misery and death that had lain on them. The smell of acid soap and putrified flesh gave Allen a queezy feeling in his stomach as he passed between the beds to the far end of the long log room.

Medical aides and what seemd to be doctors in long white coats smeared with dried blood were tending the dying and wounded from Fort Miami as Allen passed along looking for Mary Lou. When he had reached the end and still had not seen her, his first thought was that she was gone, although Hugh and the General both had assured him that she was in the hospital. He turned to go back when a voice stopped him.

"Allen! Allen! Ho-Ta-Wa!''

He spun around. There, standing in a doorway off to one side stood Mary Lou. She was pale and looked thin in the long hospital gown and her hands were white from gripping the door jam. Allen ran to her, taking her into his arms. She was crying as she clung desperately to him.

"Thank God you're here," Allen said. "Thank God that infection didn't. . . ."

He broke off and gently helped her to her bed, tenderly coaxing her not to talk. He knew at that moment that he would never leave her even if it meant going back to Boston.

But soon she spoke. "Are you all right? I was so frightened!"

Allen smiled, the grey eyes crinkling. "I'm fine. I'm just fine. Where's Aaron and Danielle?"

"They're over at Mrs. Langston's cabin. She's the doctor's wife. They're fine, although they've been askin' for you." She touched his cheek. "Hugh told me what you had to do to get Danielle back to us. You could of been killed. How did you do it?"

"You and that little girl and boy mostly, but I told you I was a right lucky fellar."

Mary Lou smiled. "Well, I'm very glad you're here now." She tenderly cradled his face in her hands and kissed him. Doctor Langston had entered, and stood near the door. Finally he cleared his throat, and Allen stood, blushing deeply. The Doctor smiled as Allen excused himself.

"Is that the celebrated Allen Crosstree, Ma'am? They're talkin' all over the Fort about how he helped you and your children."

Mary Lou was blushing now. "Yes. That's him. That's Ho-Ta-Wa."

For months, the drums spoke. "Ho-Ta-Wa enters your land—he and his squaw and his man-child and his squaw-child. Let him pass in peace, for he is of Em-O-Tee-Tee." Even the drums beyond the great mountains carried the message.

Then one day, months of moons later, a message came traveling towards the new sun—a strange message that said, "Ho-Ta-Wa and his squaw and his man-child and squaw-child have made a home in the forests on the bank of the great ocean of the setting sun." And Hugh Applegate slowly rose from the steps where he sat in the sun in Fort Wayne, on the Saint Joe, listened, and smiled.

THE END